The Whole Sky Full of Stars

Also by René Saldaña, Jr.

Finding Our Way
The Jumping Tree

The Whole Sky Full of Stars

RENÉ SALDAÑA, JR.

WENDY
LAMB
BOOKS

Published by Wendy Lamb Books
an imprint of Random House Children's Books
a division of Random House, Inc.
New York

This is a work of fiction. Names, characters, places, and incidents either are the product of the author's imagination or are used fictitiously. Any resemblance to actual persons, living or dead, events, or locales is entirely coincidental.

Text copyright © 2007 by René Saldaña, Jr.
Jacket photography © 2007 by Ericka O'Rourke

WENDY LAMB BOOKS and colophon are trademarks of Random House, Inc.

www.randomhouse.com/teens

Educators and librarians, for a variety of teaching tools, visit us at
www.randomhouse.com/teachers

Library of Congress Cataloging-in-Publication Data

Saldaña, René.
The whole sky full of stars / René Saldaña, Jr.
p. cm.
Summary: Eighteen-year-old Barry competes in a non-sanctioned boxing
match in hopes of helping his recently-widowed mother, unaware that his best
friend and manager, Alby, has his own desperate need for a share of the purse
that may put their friendship on the line.
ISBN: 978-0-385-73053-2 (trade) — ISBN: 978-0-385-90078-2 (glb)
[1. Boxing—Fiction. 2. Gambling—Fiction. 3. Friendship—Fiction.
4. Fathers and sons—Fiction. 5. Single-parent families—Fiction.
6. Mexican Americans—Fiction. 7. Texas—Fiction.] I. Title.
PZ7.S149Who 2007
[Fic]—dc22   2006026698

Printed in the United States of America

10 9 8 7 6 5 4 3 2 1

First Edition

for Kristina Ann Saldaña,
the fire of my heart, woman of my life

and

for Lukas Frederick René,
a book all his own

also for Mikah Sven Elias,
our second book

for Milton

The Whole Sky Full of Stars

one

Alby didn't even see it coming. One second he was standing in his yard talking to his best friend: "Barry, I overheard a couple of guys at school talking; they said that for an older lady, your momma's still got it going, if you know what I mean—"; the next second there was Barry's fist on Alby's nose and the pain and shooting lights that came with it. He crumpled to the ground.

Alby tried to get hold of himself. How had it happened? He hadn't even seen Barry cock back his arm, nor the look in the eyes a guy gets when he's about to punch your lights out.

"Am I bleeding?" Alby hid his nose in his hands. "Man, Barry, I was just telling you what I heard. What's your problem?" Alby rolled onto his side and shook his head. "Stars. You've got me seeing the whole sky full of stars."

Barry stretched out his hand to his buddy. *Why'd he have to bring Momma into this?* Barry thought. *Talking about her like she's some kind of a . . .* He couldn't even finish the thought. His buddy bringing his momma down with that sort of gutter talk. But was it reason enough to punch your best friend? After all, Alby was just the messenger.

"What kind of friend pops a buddy on the schnozz for no good reason?" Still, Alby took Barry's hand, stood, and brushed the dirt and grass from the seat of his pants. "Can I trust you to swipe this junk off my back without whacking me?"

A thought was beginning to take shape in Alby's head.

"Yeah." Barry wiped Alby's back, then pulled a twig from his hair. "You know, maybe a friend shouldn't talk about another's momma," said Barry. He'd never hit a person outside of his sparring partner at the gym or that one time Pop let his guard down, training in the garage. He'd always wondered whether he'd be able to knock someone down with one blow. Here was his answer. Alby was smaller, but he had a big mouth on him. "Anyway, sorry if it hurt."

"If? If? It hurt like a mean dog, man. What's your problem? We've known each other a long time, Bare. You've got to know I didn't mean no disrespect." He touched his nose. "From now on, I got it, your momma's off limits. But still, popping me like that? Anyway, I'm sorry too."

And now, Alby's idea had taken shape. *Man! Barry sure*

can hit. If I can just talk him into putting these boxing skills to good use, it could be a win-win situation for the both of us. He'd seen an ad in the paper a couple of days ago. "That was a solid smack—one shot, and I went down. I've always thought you were tough, but that tough? All that training you did with your pop—it's paying out. *Ching, ching, ching.*" Alby made like he was pulling the arm of a slot machine.

Barry picked at the broken skin on a knuckle. His fists, wide like Pop's, were scarred from hitting the bags for so long. He and Pop had been training in the garage since he was in the fifth grade, then in the gym for a few months before Pop died. Barry looked at Alby, who was rubbing the bridge of his nose. Lately, Alby had started using gambling lingo: *paying out* like those one-armed bandits in Vegas would do: *ching, ching, ching.* This kind of talk wasn't like Alby. But Alby'd been acting strange. He'd even started dressing in flashier clothes: black button-downs, tan slacks, dress shoes, and sunglasses that he usually wore across the top of his slicked-back hair.

"You know what this means? You're ready." Alby was pacing back and forth, talking with his hands.

"Ready for what?"

"We need to get you into that Man o' Might competition coming into town in a week. I read about it in the paper. I'll look it up online to make sure."

"What are you talking about?"

"You fight good. You still working out, right?" said Alby. He couldn't have planned it any better.

"Sure. Not at the gym. At home I'm working the bags, lifting weights, running ten miles. But are you nuts?" Barry said. "Those kinds of fights are more like brawls. I've heard stories of people fighting and then keeling over two or three days later." Even as he spoke, he imagined himself climbing into the ring, his name being called out, the crowd chanting "Barry, Barry," drowning out his opponent's introduction. Then he saw himself bobbing and weaving, quick-footed, stepping out of the way of a reckless punch and countering with a one-two combination, stunning his opponent just long enough to land a blow square on the liver, one that would bring him down for good. He could see the announcer holding his hand up in the air in victory, wrapping a champion's belt around Barry's waist. He'd be the people's champion.

But no. This event Alby was talking about was more like a rock 'em, sock 'em clash between guys with chips on their shoulders who needed to prove something to somebody, who dreamed of big prize money. *All the wrong reasons to fight.* "Sorry, Alby. I can't."

"Oh, come on, with a whacker like that, you got the makings of a champ, like your pop used to say. No one would get close enough to you to hurt you. They'd have to watch out for you."

Barry's brow wrinkled.

Quick, Alby said, "Tell you what—I'll manage you. There's good money to be made. Big payouts. Easy money.

Whatever we make we'll split sixty-forty, heavy on your end, of course. What do you say?"

Barry cocked his head. There it was again: "easy money," "sixty-forty split," and "heavy on your end." *Who talks that way?* He shook his head. "No way." Barry and Pop had been planning on him trying out for the school's boxing team when he got to be a junior, then seeing where it took him. They knew Momma was dead set against Barry fighting, but Pop had trained some good fighters in Mexico in his youth. Two years ago, he'd said, "Mi'jo, you're a natural. I think you're ready. Together, I know we can talk your momma into it. She just doesn't want to see you get hurt. We'll start up slow at the gym downtown. Do it right. That way she'll see she's got nothing to worry about." But Barry had quit thinking about all this when Pop died last year. There were more important things in life, like helping Momma with the bills. Pop's life insurance had run out quick, and so had his savings. *Could that be why I slugged Alby? I just hate seeing her so tired; worse, I've got no clue how to help her out.*

Alby knew he'd have a hard row ahead talking Barry into fighting. Barry was big and solid, a good three inches taller than Alby, and outweighed him by thirty pounds easy. Barry could probably beat anybody his own size or bigger, but he was a teddy bear. Then there was the churchgoing business: twice every Sunday, once on Wednesday—God is love; showing kindness to a neighbor, etc. Still, Barry hadn't turned the other cheek just now. And *why* hadn't he?

Because of his momma. Because of what Alby said about her. Best he could tell, Barry was still learning how to be the man of the house. With his pop dead, Barry was touchy about taking care of his momma.

Alby stopped fooling with his nose. That was it. That would be the route Alby would take. He knew Barry would do anything for his mother, and almost anything for his best pal. *So how do I convince him?*

Alby was in trouble. He should've known better than to get involved with a cardsharp like Ciro, probably the oldest senior in school since he'd been kept back at least twice. Ciro was a loan shark, giving guys at school a month to pay him back without interest, and if they didn't they'd get another month, but this time with fifteen percent tacked on. Always there was the threat of a beating from Ciro's thugs. He also ran a poker night over at his folks' house—just a folding table in the center of the garage-turned-club, music blaring, Ciro's strong-arms guarding the half-lowered door from outsiders. Alby had gotten all excited watching the poker tournaments on TV: guys in shiny jackets sitting around the table, their hair combed back, wearing sunglasses under the bright camera lights. Stacks of chips in front of them. So, a couple of months back, he couldn't resist Ciro's invitation to play. When Alby walked in, he thought, *This has to be how those TV guys feel, light-headed and tingly. Ready to dance with Lady Luck.*

That good feeling didn't last long. At first, he'd been getting just the right cards, almost like he was being allowed to win. When he had a pile of chips, Alby said, "It's getting late, boys. I'm packing it up for the night." That was how he imagined the pros would leave a table. Then Ciro said, "Yeah, thanks for hanging out. Bobby, get our boy his money. Or, what do you think of this: we go head-to-head, double-or-nothing hand, Texas Hold 'Em? I'll even open a new deck." A slight grin crossed his broad face. Ciro had a scar running across his left cheekbone all the way to the edge of his ear.

Alby saw himself reflected in Ciro's dark glasses. *Why didn't I wear mine?*

Ciro unwrapped the cellophane on a pack. Alby nodded: *New deck, better luck.* Man, he was on a roll. He could've left with five hundred bucks; now he stood to make a thousand! How proud would Dad be? Alby'd be just like him, a moneymaker, a breadwinner. So he played one last hand.

And lost it.

Ciro said, "You know what, carnal? I feel bad. You were such a good sport, so maybe, if you want to win some of this back, I'll let you play on credit. What do you say?"

Alby'd had one good run, he could do it again, right?

He started up with a hundred dollars in borrowed chips. Lost. Borrowed more, and kept losing. For the whole rest of the night. It was his stupid bottom lip that did him in—his tell. Tells were little gestures that showed an opponent your feelings, thoughts you were trying to hide—a tic, a slight shrugging of the shoulders, a curled lip, a deep breath, a

gleam in the eyes. Tells were specially bad if you were playing cards for money with a bunch of guys who figured out
what yours were.

He walked out of Ciro's place down his original hundred
smacks and another five hundred in the hole. When he was
leaving, Ciro caught up to him: "Hold up, man. You're a
good sport. So instead of a month like I said inside, I'll give
you two to pay up." He called his boys over. "Two months.
But no longer. They'll make sure about that. Got it? Oh, and
don't tell nobody about this. Not the cops, not your mommy
or daddy, no one. It'll go bad for you, and for whoever you
blab to. Plus, you don't want to be the one responsible for
shutting me down, do you? That wouldn't be good for any
of us."

Alby looked up at Ciro's boys. Like Ciro, they'd flunked
enough classes over the years to be held back a time or
two. Alby'd heard stories: they'd slashed teachers' tires
who'd failed them, broken classroom windows, and fought
just about anyone at school who looked at them wrong.
Alby swallowed hard and said, "Yeah, Ciro. Thanks, man. I
got it."

"Just to make sure," Ciro said, and looked at his pals.
One grabbed Alby by the arms, and the other knocked the
wind out of him with a punch.

Alby doubled over, sucking in air.

"Not a soul," Ciro whispered in his ear.

No way. He would never tell anybody about this. Alby
knew Dad would pony up the cash if he'd only ask, but there

were two reasons why Alby wasn't going to do that: one, he'd have to jump through so many hoops with Dad. Dad, the top car salesman in his district. He could hear him say: "Tell me and Mom again, son, how much you lost?" Dad sitting on the couch, his suit coat still on but his tie loosened at the neck, arms crossed. All smug. "And, looking back on the game, can you pinpoint the moment you lost?" He'd want Alby to repeat every detail until he was satisfied, then he'd come up with a lesson, almost always related to car sales. If Dad made Alby guess what the moral was, he wouldn't let up until Alby got it right. Dad would want to meet this Ciro, see what kind of a crooked game he was running, maybe cut a deal of some kind for his kid. That would mean Alby had spilled the beans, which led to reason number two, the real one for not breathing a word of this: Ciro's goons would come after him *and* Dad. No way!

The deadline was a week and a half away. He'd saved up just over three hundred dollars by doing extra chores around the house and selling stuff on eBay—mostly NASCAR ball caps and toy race cars Dad had gotten signed for him at the dealership. But it was still nowhere near the five hundred. And Ciro was breathing heavy down his neck: a month after the game, Ciro's guys came around to remind him. One pulled a blade and carved crud from under his fingernails. The other scrunched the back and sides of Alby's neck so tight he almost fainted. "You think this is bad, if you don't come through wait till we come back in a month and really knock you around something fierce."

Alby had to prove he could get out of trouble just as easy as get in it. Dad was always going on about how "in this world you're either part of the problem or part of the solution. I'm teaching you something here, son. Pay attention. Don't come to me with your problems without first trying to solve them yourself. I'm a busy man; I don't get to be the top salesman of the year ten years running without working at it, or by letting the world beat me down."

Alby could've told Barry, but Ciro had said *nobody*. One-on-one, Barry could take on those goons, but they wouldn't fight fair.

They'd shown up two and a half weeks ago: "Just checking up on our investment," said the bigger one. He faked a punch, and Alby flinched. The thugs were laughing as they left.

This Man o' Might competition had to be the solution. He'd find out how much the winner would get. If the prize was, what, seven hundred and fifty bucks, he'd take his share—three hundred—plus his savings, and that would cover his debt. Alby would have Ciro meet him after the fights to pay him back what he owed. And since Alby would have the cash with him, what could it hurt to put it to use? What was Dad always saying: "To make money sometimes you've got to spend it"? Alby was sure there'd be others at the fight interested in placing a bet or two. Barry would be a no-name, so the odds would be heavy against him. Alby would put part of his savings on Barry and clean up. Maybe he would drop everything he had, all three hundred bucks, on Barry to win his first match, even money with any and all takers, doubling his stash just like that.

But what if Barry lost? Then Alby would be out every cent, and he'd still owe Ciro. He'd be in more trouble than ever.

Alby would have to recoup his losses, so he'd have to gamble with money he didn't have, which meant Barry would have to win, win, win; otherwise, tougher guys than Ciro would come after him.

Or he could ask Ciro for another loan if worse came to worst. Hope for the best.

Alby shook his head as he and Barry walked over to the porch. *Wake up! That's what got you in trouble the first time.*

But if Alby was between a rock and a hard place, he knew Barry was even more hard up: Barry and his momma were strapped for cash, and here Alby had thrown good money away. He didn't feel guilty for having it, or like he owed it to Barry to give him some, but to be so thoughtless, so careless with it—he could never tell Barry how he'd lost the money, not when Barry's momma worked two jobs just to make ends meet.

Alby'd have to play it just right, not say word one about Ciro, but *Barry, wouldn't it be the greatest to hand over a lump of cash to your momma the night you win? What a smile you'll put on her face; maybe she'll be able to take a week or two off if the prize money's big enough.* Could Alby do that? Use Barry's emotions against him?

Ugly as it sounded, this would have to be his angle.

Did he have a choice?

No.

Barry just had to fight.

"Listen," Alby said, pointing to a rocking chair on the porch, "have a seat. I'm going inside for a sec. I need to see what you did to my face." The little gears in his head were working. He'd find that ad online and print it out.

Barry watched Alby let the screen door smack hard behind him. At home, Momma would've started in: "Careful. Screen doors don't grow on trees. Unless you know of any screen door trees?" Momma never said stuff like this in an angry way; more like *I'm tired at the end of this day and still not moving ahead but two steps back.* So Barry tried to do right by her.

Barry sighed and looked across the backyard. Now, Alby, he ruled this roost from morning to night. His parents let him get away with God knows what. Alby always said, "Freedom is all it is. They know I wouldn't take advantage, really." But often he did.

Barry used to be jealous of Alby's privileges until one day Pop sat him down in the '64 Ford Galaxie they were restoring. The red car was to be Barry's graduation present. "I'm disappointed in you, mi'jo. The principal called," Pop said. "Mrs. Castillo told me you and Alby were caught trying to roll a cigarette in the boys' room."

Barry was close to crying. "This is not the way to earn your car." Pop was in the driver's seat, his hands on the wheel. "And if I know Alby's father, he's going to try to talk 'man to man' with that boy, try to talk some sense into Alby's head instead of taking care of the matter like a dad should. It's right there in the Bible: raise a boy in the right way, and he'll grow up to be the apple of your eye." Pop seemed embarrassed for Alby's dad, Mr. Alonzo. As he spoke, he kept looking at his hands gripping the steering wheel. Then he turned to Barry. "Our family's not that way, mi'jo. You understand? We take responsibility for the bad stuff; we take credit for the good. Take King David in the Old Testament, for example. He murdered a man because he wanted the other man's wife. Suffered in so many ways, as a result. But he fessed up to God. Or Muhammad Ali—good old Cassius Clay. Chose not to fight in Vietnam. Lost his title for it. He passed up some great opportunities in the ring. But it was the principle of the matter for him. Here are two men who never balked at doing the right thing, even when the odds were against them."

Barry got the picture, so he told Pop what his punishment should be. A long time ago, he learned to decide the best course of action for his folks to take in disciplining him. He never hedged. This time, he told Pop, "I've dishonored you and Momma. I'm sorry. I got no excuse, other than I was being stupid. For that, I should mow the lawn, straighten up the garage, and wash the truck for no allowance." Pop nodded. They got out of the Galaxie and went to the kitchen. Pop made them ham and cheese sandwiches, prayed over the food, then said, "What's first, mowing, cleaning up, or washing?"

So what would Pop have said about this Man o' Might fighting business? More important, what would he have said about Barry slugging Alby, a much smaller guy, for disrespecting Momma? Probably "It's not something I'd condone normally, mi'jo—fighting's for the ring. But there are times like this one I don't mind you stepping up like that. Alby should have known better than to talk like that about your momma. She's a boatload of rubies." Sitting on the porch, Barry thought, *Yes, she is, Pop. You couldn't be more right.*

Every Saturday for a year now, she'd gotten up early, well before work, to cut flowers from her garden or buy some at the supermarket. Then they'd visit the gravesite. She'd replace last week's flowers, weed the plot, and brush clean Pop's headstone, which read, *Blessed Is the Man. . . .*

She was still wearing black on Sundays, and she pinned a brooch with a picture of Pop on whatever she wore to work. Her hair had gone from dark brown to dull brown streaked with gray in this last year, and her shoulders sagged a bit. *But boy,* Barry thought, *she's still the beautiful woman of her wedding pictures.* If only she smiled more often. Even at the end, when Pop spent most of his last month bedridden and medicated, in and out of a hard sleep, she was all smiles for him. Then he died, and the smile was gone.

Alby came out of the house with a pitcher of lemonade and two glasses of ice cubes. Under his arm was the Man o' Might flyer. He set everything on a little table, filled the glasses, and passed one to Barry. He unfolded the flyer and snapped a finger on it: "Hot off the presses."

Barry didn't turn.

Alby said, "Here you go, Bare. Here's what I'm talking about. It's a boxing extravaganza; all boxing, all night; and the main event, they call it the Battle in the Fence o' Fighting. Probably like we've seen in wrestling; they'll put up a chain-link fence around the ring to make it more exciting, and last man standing wins the whole enchilada. Can you see it, Barry? You can be the champ, I bet you."

Barry took the flyer. It would be nice to hand Momma his part of the winnings. And show Pop that all that training hadn't been wasted. He'd set his trophy on the mantel next to the picture of Pop as a young man and Fabian Mercado, one of the boys Pop trained in Mexico. Fabian had just won his first amateur fight and he was sharing the spotlight with Pop, holding Pop's arm up. There was also a postcard that came when Fabian was on the verge of challenging for the WBC welterweight title. It was a shot of Fabian in a boxing pose, staring into the camera, a scowl on his face, not one hair out of place. He'd written across the bottom half, "To Bartolomeo, Fabian 'El Mero Mero' Mercado."

That was where Barry's trophy would go. He smiled.

Alby thought, *I've got him looking, at least.*

two

Alby and Barry met in the first grade. Barry was the new boy. One day he peed his pants. Alby raised his hand and said, "Miss Peters, uh, can you come here and see something, please?"

Miss Peters walked up to his desk. "What do you need?"

Alby pointed with his eyes at Barry's wet pants, a finger to his lips. The big-headed boy was looking down at his hands covering his lap, sniffling. Alby didn't want anybody else to smell the pee and make fun of the new boy.

But with the teacher asking that question so loud, all the others turned to look. A few pointed and laughed. And that made Alby angry.

Miss Peters whispered something to Barry, then said, "Okay, children, let's set our pencils down and line up outside the door. We're going on a little treasure hunt. The prize is a Hershey Bar." Everybody jumped up.

One boy came down the aisle and said to Barry, "Pee Boy, Pee Boy, ha ha ha ha!" Alby put out his foot and tripped him.

Barry glared at Alby, so Alby got up and headed outside.

When all the kids had lined up against the wall, the teacher said, "Grab a partner, and first, let's go look for a reddish-brown rock the size of a dime. First one back with it gets one point. Okay, go." Everyone ran off. But not Alby. He noticed Barry hadn't gotten up from his desk, so he pulled Miss Peters off to the side and whispered, "Hey, Miss, how about the new boy?"

"Never mind about him, Alberto. He'll come out when he's ready. You go with the others."

"Sure," he said. But he stayed near the classroom door and turned dirt and pebbles over with his foot instead until Miss Peters and his classmates were busy scanning the yard.

When the door creaked open, Alby hid behind a mesquite and saw Barry run for the bathroom. Alby followed and waited at a picnic table. He felt bad. Maybe if he'd kept his mouth shut, then no one would know about the pee? Maybe no one would have ever found out? But he had called the teacher over. *Stupid, stupid, stupid!*

Alby walked over to the bathroom, thinking about saying he was sorry. He didn't notice Barry stick his head out the door, and he ran right into the new boy, who was much bigger than he was.

Instead of apologizing, he ran away and hid behind the mesquite again.

After school, a kid on the bus yelled at Barry, "Hey, Pee Boy."

Barry buried his chin in his chest and quickly found a seat near the front.

"His name's Barry!" Alby said. "And he's my friend, so stop."

"Pee Boy—"

Alby knocked the kid in the face, and they tussled until the bus driver tore them apart.

Barry never forgot what Alby'd done.

That was what Alby was counting on today.

three

Barry took a swig of his lemonade and thought, *How can I say no to my best friend? It's what I've been training for, kind of. And Alby's right: my chances are better than average, if I say so myself. Still, it seems like Alby's got his reasons for me to fight, but he's not saying. An easy buck? I'll be the one doing the hard work. What will Alby be doing—managing? I don't need him for that. There's got to be more to this than he's letting on.* "Alby?"

"Yeah, Bare?"

"How long've we known each other?"

"Bare, if that's not the dumbest question, I don't know what is. You know—first grade. That's a long time. Why?"

"Never mind." Barry refilled their glasses. "Anyway, about the Man o' Might—"

"Yeah?" Alby leaned in.

"Well, it's a stupid idea, first. How many people do you think will enter? Let's say twenty-five. That's a lot of fighting to do for a measly what?" He took a look at the flyer again. Turned it over and back. "It doesn't even say how much I'd win. Don't get me wrong, now. I sure could use sixty percent of one hundred dollars, but how likely is it that I get past the first round? I mean, who would I be fighting? Grown men. Guys stronger, bigger than me. Better trained? Not likely, but still, I've never been in a real fight." Even as he spoke, Barry knew he would do well. He was a pretty good fighter. But this wasn't the kind of boxing he and Pop had been training for. They'd been talking Golden Gloves, maybe even the Olympic trials after a couple of years of amateur bouts. This Man o' Might probably wasn't sanctioned, and the fighters wouldn't be pros, but they wouldn't be amateurs, either. They'd be regular Joes fighting for a chance at the prize. And what was this Fence o' Fighting thing? It sounded scary, like he could get hurt. He took a sip of his lemonade. "Second, what do you need cash for? Back in middle school you told me your folks gave you big bucks for an allowance."

Alby ripped the flyer away from Barry. "You don't know what you're talking about, man. Money doesn't last forever, you know. It's meant for spending: school clothes, shoes, tennis shoes. Homecoming. It disappears. And what business is it of yours, really, what I need cash for? Maybe I just do. Maybe I don't. So what of it?"

"That's exactly it. Cash has never been an issue for you. You need it, your folks give it to you."

"Listen, my finances are none of your concern, you understand? I said the cut's sixty-forty. That's an extra twenty for you of none of your business."

Alby was off his chair now, spitting as he talked. He'd never spoken like this to Barry, at least not about money.

Barry said, "Settle down, bud. No need to get your underpants in a wad. Let's talk this through, yeah?"

"What's there to talk about? I see us making some good money, quick and easy, and you're being a pain in the neck about it, *bud*. On your all high and mighty horse. Like I'm the one with money woes." *This is low*, he thought, *what I'm about to do.* He wouldn't be lying exactly, just avoiding the truth by a hair. "All this time I'm thinking of you—" Alby hesitated, then thought of Ciro's goons. "I'm thinking of your momma, too."

Barry started to get up.

"Hold on a minute. I don't mean anything disrespectful. I learned that lesson earlier today, thank you very much." Alby pointed at his nose.

Barry eased down, took back his lemonade, but didn't drink.

"Here's what I'm saying, Bare—" Alby started pacing up and down the porch. "Everybody in the neighborhood knows she works and works and never complains."

Barry had to shake his head at that one. Boy, did she

ever complain: "Two jobs, fourteen-hour days, five, some-times six days out of the week, and what do we have to show for it? I barely get the bills paid; one step forward, three back it feels like to me; it can't go on like this too much longer. It's been nothing but catch-up since . . ." Then she'd cry some, lock herself in their room, hers and Pop's, and cry some more. There'd be nothing Barry could do but rest his back up against the wall next to the bedroom door and wait. When she came out, he'd hug her tight, say everything was going to be all right. How he'd quit running, lifting weights, and training on the bags. He'd mow more lawns on week-ends, afternoons, too. Then she'd say, "It isn't fair that you've got to do all this yard work for diddly-squat when you should be on the basketball team instead." *She complains*, he thought. *Alby's got no idea*.

Alby was still talking. Barry had missed most of it.

Alby saw that Barry had a look in his eyes like he was thinking about his momma, maybe his pop, too. Alby knew he was close to convincing him. He stopped walking back and forth, his back to Barry. He ran his hand through his black hair and breathed deep. He felt crummy, but he had to do it. He spun around. "So you see, Bare, we've got to think about your momma. You mean she couldn't use the break? You're the one always saying 'Honor your mother and father.' Look me in the eyes, and honest to God tell me that passing up a chance to be so helpful is honorable." He waited to see if tacking on something from the Bible had done the trick. He leaned in, placed a hand on Barry's shoulder, and whispered, "This is a good thing, pal. I mean, how is it it's me thinking of doing this for your momma and not you?" A line appeared between Barry's eyebrows. His friend's tell gave it all away. Barry did that thing with the eyebrows when he was thinking hard.

Alby said, "No way you're that callous. She's all you've got left."

Barry's face went slack, distant.

Alby knew: he didn't know when to stop talking sometimes. Mentioning death was off limits. He removed his hand and grabbed the pitcher. "You want more?"

Barry waved the pitcher away. *This is about money, plain and simple,* he thought. In his gut, Barry knew this wasn't about stretching forth a helping hand to anybody but Alby. Alby was a hustler, "able to sell ice to an Eskimo," he'd said about himself once.

"Sorry again about the nose." Barry stood, went down the steps of the back porch, and headed toward his own house just across the canal. Usually, the walk home was good for quieting his thoughts.

Pop was on his mind.

※

Barry had been gone a few minutes when Alby heard Dad walk into the house: "Babe, Alberto. You guys home? I got something for the both of you. Come see what it is."

Alby didn't budge.

"Is that you out on the porch, Sport?"

Alby didn't like being called Alberto or Sport or bud. Why couldn't Dad call him *mi'jo* like Barry's pop? They never hung out in the family room playing pool or on the PlayStation. They didn't have an old car to work on. Their two-car garage was spic-and-span, not a thing out of place, no oil spots on the floor. Alby's dad didn't train him at boxing, or anything else. Dad lived and breathed car sales. At home, during commercials, he'd let Alby and his mom know what he'd sold, to whom, and for how much. He'd rub his hands together and start in on one of those silly speeches on success in life, quoting passages from Lee Iacocca's book on how to sell cars.

This afternoon, Dad was home earlier than usual for what he called "an eat-and-run" dinner. Then he'd zip on back to the car lot to meet a client, "and this sale will put me over the top for the month."

When no one answered, Dad peeked his head out the screen door. "It is you? Hey, look at this." He walked out onto the porch, poured himself lemonade in Barry's glass, plunked down beside Alby, and handed over a bag. "This one's yours, and that one's your mom's. Go ahead. Look in it." His smile couldn't get any bigger.

Not that I'd think of ratting Ciro out, but just once, can't Dad see there's something bothering me? "Maybe later, Dad." Alby started to get up.

"Where you going, Sport? I got this especially for you."

Alby looked in the bag. "Oh, a cap. Thanks, Dad. I'll add it to the others."

"It isn't just any old cap, bud. It's autographed by none other than Jeff Gordon. This one's made out to you, see?" He pulled the cap out and turned it over to show the bottom of the bill. "I sent him the caps a couple of months ago, a box with return postage, and a note reminding him we'd met in the pits last year at the Texas Motor Speedway. I'd almost forgotten I'd done it. So when they came in today, I got all excited. Do you like it?"

Alby took the cap without looking at the signature and said, "Yeah, sure, Dad. It's awesome." He stood and went up to his bedroom, sat at his computer, and signed on to the Internet. *I don't even like stupid NASCAR. What's he thinking? But—look at it this way: I got something else to sell.* He spun around and tossed the cap into his closet.

four

Alby's stupid idea had gotten Barry thinking about his pop, who was so out of it the month before he died. Because of all the treatments, he was bald and bloated in the face, though the rest of him was skinny. Nothing like the man he used to be—jet-black hair, thin but strong, full of life. That last month took a toll on Momma and Barry. But as long as Pop was alive, they kept up a cheery front.

Two weeks before Pop passed away, he and Barry were in the garage. Barry was shadowboxing in the corner over by the punching bag. Pop sat on an old upright tire, stooped at the shoulders. He'd been coming out to the garage when he felt up to it. All along, he said he would beat this cancer. If Barry'd known Pop was that close to the end, he would've gone over and held on tight.

Man, Pop was lucid that night. His eyes focused in on Barry, he reached out for him, and clear as day, said, "Hey, mi'jo, it's all about the fundamentals. You've got to keep working out on the bag. Go hard at it. Just when you think you're close to the edge, go farther. You enjoy a victory best when you work for it."

"Yeah, Pop, I will, every chance I get."

"Remember it's the jab to the nose first, then a combo to the chest and down to the gut. If you can get at the liver, that's the best." He blinked a few times, jerked slightly, and looked around like he was lost. Then the cobwebs cleared.

Barry walked over to Pop.

It was a tumor in the head that had done this, but Pop's voice sounded so strong just then it made Barry think he *would* get better. Pop was wearing the Broncs baseball cap Barry'd gotten for him the last time they went to one of the university's games. Barry said, "Hey, Pop. When do you want to get back to my old junker? No one'll buy it in this condition." He meant the cool Galaxie Pop had bought for him from a man in South Carolina. "It still needs some tinkering. I've been piddling away at it after my workouts, but what do I know about—what do you call the engine—a Police Interceptor?"

Two years ago, Pop and Barry had seen the car advertised in a classic cars magazine. Pointing to the photo, Pop had said, "This is the ride I would've bought back in the day, mi'jo, if I had had the money. The kind of car I would've been proud to take on a first date with your momma. It'll never go out of style. Just look at it." Barry agreed. It was a slick car. They'd taken a bus overnight to Greenville, South Carolina, to look at it.

The owner, an old man, was waiting for them at the station. On the way to see the car, he said, "It's the hardest thing to sell it, because it's the car my wife and me drove off in right after our wedding. It's a beaut. But I'm no spring chicken, and the Galaxie's a car for a young man." He looked at Barry, who could see himself behind that wheel cruising to the high school nice and slow, the windows rolled down. All the girls asking to ride with him.

The Galaxie was parked in the old man's workshop, under a tarp. Pop walked around it slowly a couple of times, stooping close, then squinting. "It's in fair enough shape," Pop had said. "Hubcaps are missing. I see some of the interior leather's cracked. It'll need new paint. The chrome's decent." He got on his knees and knocked on the gas tank with his knuckles. "But no rust anywhere. Can we take it for a spin?"

Pop stopped at red lights and listened to the engine. He waited a second or two after the light turned green and then went. On a straightaway, he stepped hard on the gas and got it up to eighty-five before slowing down. "What do you think, mi'jo? Is it something you would drive?"

Barry smiled and said, "Sure. Like the man said, it's a beaut. Can I test it?"

Pop shook his head: "Not until it's ours. Maybe on the trip back."

When they pulled into the old man's driveway, Pop was trying to hide his excitement, but the corners of his mouth kept curling up. This was the car they'd been saving up for, what Pop called Barry's "college fund, a real investment," the car they'd work on together and sell for a good price when the time was right. Pop paid six thousand dollars cash. Driving south on I-85, Barry asked, "Why didn't you try to talk him down on the price, Pop?"

Pop ran his arched fingers up and around the steering wheel, smiling big. "When you know something's worth it, there's no making deals. Like the ad said: *it's got potential.*"

Just outside of Atlanta, they stopped for gas and snacks. When Barry got back from the restroom, Pop said, "What do you think?" pointing at the rearview mirror. Hanging there were a pair of red mini–boxing gloves. "They were next to the register; I couldn't resist." Every once in a while, Pop reached over and flicked them, sending them swinging; he was a kid with a new toy.

Pop worked as a mechanic at a foreign auto shop in McAllen and then came home from that job and worked in his own garage on American cars. Usually Barry held a light for Pop, whose legs always stuck out from under a T-Bird or Mustang. The Galaxie was for after business hours.

For Barry, passing wrenches and sockets to Pop was where he wanted to be most in the whole world. But since Pop got sick, they'd been working on the Galaxie less and less.

That last night in the garage, Barry looked down. The

dirt floor of the garage was soaked in oil from years of fixing trucks and cars. How many histories had seeped deep into the ground? As many of them as the layers of oil he and Alby found when they used to dig into the dirt.

"Pop," he said, "about the car?"

Pop's eyes lit up like he was going to beat this thing and get back to his old life: family, work, their car. Then he said, "I don't know, mi'jo. I don't think I'm going to make it here."

Barry was stunned. Pop hadn't talked like this before.

His voice cracking, Barry said, "Don't you say stuff like that. You'll live longer than the moon. You'll outlast me, even." He didn't want to cry. It'd be like he was giving in. He swallowed hard and looked evenly at Pop.

He knelt and held Pop's hand. Pop motioned for Barry to lean in, then said in Spanish: "Mi'jo, you're not a boy anymore. No longer your mom's and my Little Man. It's all on your shoulders now." Then he switched back to English: "In the ring, a fighter's got to be focused on nothing else but the man in front of him. He starts paying attention to something else, he'll get popped hard. Remember that—always alert, always paying attention. Don't get caught with anything." Pop pointed a finger at the air in front of him and said, "Winning doesn't always look like winning, Fabian. And there's more important things than fame and money. Take Job in the Bible, for example. Lost everything, but in the end God smiled down on him. He was a true champ. You get me, mi'jo?"

Barry was confused. First, why had Pop just called him Fabian, the fighter he'd trained long ago? His name had never come up in any of their conversations. He'd only heard stories from Momma about one of the kids Pop knew in Mexico years before he made his way to Texas. "Fabian had it all, according to your pop," she said. "He was moving up in the amateur ranks; had what it took to medal in the Olympics for Mexico. But he wanted to do more than amateur boxing. He wanted to make a living at it. He couldn't wait, he said. But Pop kept at him about how good he was, how one day if he was patient he'd be a world champ and make money hand over fist." Unbeknownst to Pop, Fabian began betting on himself to win or lose, and made a good bit of money. "Of course," Momma continued, "this was illegal. When your pop found out, he was devastated. Instead of turning the boy in to the boxing commission, he found Fabian a manager in the pro ranks, and left Monterrey for good." Apparently, Pop had been accused of betting on his own man too, but Momma said it was a lie. "Your pop would never do that. It still hurts him. Your pop, who would never, ever gamble!"

And why was Pop switching back and forth between Spanish and English? Pop always insisted that Barry speak English at home. "The moment your grandparents, my brothers, sisters, and I arrived in the U.S., I realized that if a man was going to get educated and make money in this country, then English it had to be. That, and hard work. Sweat." Pop only spoke Spanish with Barry's grandma, who had never bothered to learn English.

And why was he talking about Barry now being in charge and boxing?

Something was up, so Barry paid careful attention that last day in the garage.

Pop went on in Spanish: "Take care of my Luisa. You hear me? You take care of your momma." He was crying, and Barry buried his face in the back of Pop's hand. "A true champ's not a showboat. He's about getting down to business. Those show-offs, they're nothing but a cancer on the sport." He was quiet for a moment. Then he said, "That car's beautiful. But it's not the be-all and end-all. Just a way to pass time with you, mi'jo. It was good, right, boy?"

"The best," Barry said, kissing Pop's hand. There was grease under Pop's fingernails. As a kid, Barry thought they were that color for real.

"Cuidala bien. Y si un dia—"

Pop took a deep breath, and Barry looked up. What else was he going to say? "Take care of her. And if one day—"

If one day, what?

But Pop didn't say.

Barry had to take a hard look to make sure Pop was all right.

Pop had a smile on his face. He pointed to the Galaxie and said, "The car's yours. Do whatever you want with it. And you're right—all those times were the best. I'm just sorry I can't work on it with you."

Barry stood. "Pop, let's go inside. Momma's probably putting dinner on the table."

"Yep." But Pop didn't move. Instead, he wiped away his tears. "Dust in my eyes. Momma'll think I've been crying like a baby."

Barry smiled and took Pop by the elbow and helped him up.

Pop ran a hand over the hood of the car and smiled. "Here you go, mi'jo." He handed Barry the keys. "Help me cover it. But quick; I'm hungry. Good. Now let's get out of here."

Two weeks later, he died in the hospital.

Barry and Momma were by his side. Barry didn't hear the noises of the machines falter, then go flat to a droning beep; he didn't see the lights flashing in a different pattern. He kept holding Pop's hand and staring at Pop's clean finger-nails. Then the nurses came and he had to let go of Pop's hand. And he hadn't found out what it was Pop wanted him to know or do in case one day . . .

He'd have to figure that out on his own.

five

Tonight, Barry found the house empty. It was close to seven, and Momma would be working till ten or even midnight, depending on whether Jimmy showed up for his shift. If not, who but Momma knew how to run the shrink-wrap machine?

He looked in the fridge and like always found a plate covered in foil, the dinner she had made for him that morning.

Barry got to bed late. She still hadn't come home. She'd be so tired and dragging, sleep a few hours, and then head to the other job, home for an early dinner and a change of clothes, then on to the night one. It was never-ending, and it was taking its toll, a different sort than during Pop's last months alive; the change then, Barry had noticed, was more in her heart. She hadn't smiled much, or laughed like she used to. Working nonstop was a different kind of eating away; she had lost a lot of weight, the tips of her fingers and her knuckles had red spots like burns, and she walked slower, stooped.

He lay in bed, thinking. *The Man o' Might's a stupid thing, really.* But he pictured coming home with that cash, putting it in her hands, saying, "Momma, why don't you take a week off, maybe two; rest? It's on me." Still, as Alby would say, the odds were heavy against him, so why was Alby pushing him so hard, bringing up Momma, too? *What is it going on with him?*

※

Alby couldn't sleep either. Not for lack of trying. He'd roll onto his stomach, then turn over onto his back, hands clasped behind his head, staring at the black ceiling.

He was thinking over the pounding he'd already gotten and was going to get. Ciro's muscle always wore black T-shirts. When they'd shown up at Alby's house the other day, it was lucky that his parents had been at work. One of the guys had grabbed him by the left ear and wrenched it, whispering: "Understand? Pay back, or else." One rumor about these goons was that they'd put the star linebacker on crutches because they'd heard he'd said something about them. But he really hadn't. Scary.

Alby would be hurting like he'd never hurt before. He'd

said, "I've got some of the cash. I'll show it to you if you want. I got it under my bed."

They laughed.

If only, if only he was tougher than these guys. He'd challenge them to the Fence o' Fighting match, knock them around like rag dolls. Their bodies slumped in different corners. Alby's face in the winner's photo on next year's flyer.

That reminded him: *The deadline for registration's in two days, competition's this weekend, then the money's due. Barry's just got to do this for me. What if I just told him the real reason?* He knew that Barry would agree to go through with the competition to spare Alby any pain. Barry would give Alby the shirt right off his back, and the few dollars he'd saved from mowing lawns. Except Alby'd be taking everything, *everything* from Barry, then. There was another reason: without meaning it in a bad way, Barry would probably lecture him about gambling, like he had once about how not to treat your folks. "See for yourself firsthand," he could hear Barry saying, "how betting is plain bad, and a sin, to boot." He'd quote something from the Bible about casting lots, shake his head, and frown. It wasn't so much the talking-to Alby hoped to duck, but that shake of the head. The disappointment.

He was the lowest of the lows. But . . . what other way out was there?

Another thought kept him awake: that he couldn't trust Dad with this problem. Couldn't go to him and say, "Hey, Dad, I'm in a pickle. How about some help?" Because then he'd put Dad right in the middle of it. And as with Barry, Alby'd get one of Dad's famous talks.

Now, if Barry was keeping it to himself about being dumb enough to have played cards against Ciro, Mr. Esquivel would've noticed right off and asked about it. He would've been disappointed, angry, but he would've come through for his boy. He'd fork over the money, and Barry'd do some serious work to pay it back.

But Alby's dad would just hand over the cash like it was candy, tell him something about getting in over his head, pull out a deck of cards, deal them, and show him how to really play with the big boys so next time he wouldn't lose.

Mr. Esquivel would've shaken his head at Barry and walked out to the garage to work, saying, "Right now, mi'jo, I need some time alone." And that would have been the real punishment for Barry, to be apart from his pop.

While Dad would've said, "How many cards are you taking? Dealer takes two." As for Mom, the big-time lawyer, she'd call the cops on Ciro then and there.

Not a soul, Ciro had said.

He didn't fall asleep until the sun nearly cracked the horizon.

When he awoke, he had a headache and still didn't know what to do.

six

Barry woke up dead set on telling Alby no thanks. There were better ways to make cash than to use his face as a punching bag. If he'd learned anything from Pop, it was that the really worthwhile things in life, you enjoy them more when you sweat for them. "You go to the fifteenth round for the right thing. Keep on your toes the whole way. Give it your all."

Barry went down to the kitchen. He hadn't heard Momma come in, and now she'd gone to her other job. He shook his head as he ate his cereal. *She could stand a break. Maybe . . . ?* Then he shook his head again. Alby's insistence had more to do with some tight spot *he* was in than with anything else.

In a few minutes he'd meet up with Alby to walk to

school. He'd say, "Maybe we could join forces, do a lawn in half the time it takes me, then go to the next, and the one after that, and split what we make. You use your half however you want. What do you say?" Maybe Barry should offer to take the same deal as the Man o' Might thing: sixty-forty, because Barry would do all the heavy labor and Alby would amble about and say, "Let's hurry this up, why don't we?" Later, he'd argue, "It just seems wrong sort of that I'm getting the shorter end of the money stick. We *are* doing the same amount of work. Wouldn't it be more fair if we cut the purse down the middle?" Or he might say, "Of course I did less work. I got paid considerably fewer greenbacks. Duh." But even that'd be better than fighting in the match.

Barry rinsed his bowl and opened the fridge to get the lunch Momma left him for school. It wasn't there. *She didn't have time to fix lunch for herself even*, he thought. *Something's got to give.*

He turned to see her come into the kitchen. She was in her nightgown and her hair was a sleepy mess. "Morning, Barry."

"What's wrong? You sick? You taking a day? You need it, that's for sure."

She shuffled over to the table.

"I'll get you some cereal."

She sat there, her face in her hands.

"You all right? You need me to stay home?"

"No, honey," she answered. "Today they only need me for a couple of hours. So I slept in."

How old she looked this morning. End-of-the-rope tired. "Momma, everything'll be okay. You'll see."

She tried to smile.

"Trust me. Pop said, 'Mi'jo, take care of your momma,' and that's what's going to happen. Nothing to worry over. I'll figure it out for us." He kissed her on the cheek and hugged her good. "Don't worry. You just enjoy these hours off."

"What about your lunch?"

"Never mind. I said rest." He kissed her again.

She squeezed his hand.

He knew what he had to do.

✳

Barry went around Alby's house and toward the driveway.

Alby's mom met Barry on her way back to the front porch with the morning papers. She was wearing one of her power suits, the gray-striped one that matched Mr. Alonzo's. She'd pulled her hair back so tight Barry wondered if her head hurt. "Barry," she said, looking at the headlines.

"Morning, Mrs. A." He looked toward the street. "Don't tell me he slept through the alarm again?"

"Not this morning. Oddest thing—he was up at the crack of dawn. Even before Mr. Alonzo, if you can believe that."

"So, where is he, then?"

"He left for school. Something about a project?"

"Really?" asked Barry. He would've said, "That's news to me. I'm in the same classes, and no teacher assigned any special projects lately." But he was no snitch. Mrs. A would worry then. No matter what Alby said about his folks not caring one way or the other where he was, with whom, what he did till Lord knows what hours of the night, Mr. and Mrs. Alonzo did care. He remembered a time not so long ago when Alby called his mom at work because he was sick. She left in the middle of a deposition to pick him up and stayed home the rest of the day.

Barry said, "I'll see him there. Have a good day at work, then," and trotted off, hoping she wouldn't ask, "Where's your project?"

It must be something big for him to outright lie like this. They told each other everything. *This has got to do with why he wants me to fight so bad.* Barry looked up the street. *Something's wrong. Alby never gets to school early.*

He ran all the way there.

seven

Alby heard Barry calling from down the hall just as Ciro and his boys appeared around the corner. Alby waved Barry off and said to Ciro, "Hey, buddy. What's shaking?"

"Hey, buddy yourself, cockroach." He wrapped a heavy arm around Alby's shoulders. "What's this? Run into a door?" he said, pinching Alby's swollen nose, laughing it up.

Alby grimaced; Barry's punch still hurt. "It's nothing—"

"Look, fellas," Ciro said, cutting him off, "our boy here's got a zit coming in then." They all laughed. Then Ciro gripped Alby's shoulder. "Time's running out. You told my boys you had a fair amount of the action you owe me. Why not buy yourself an extra week by handing that cash over now?"

Alby remembered his one tell: every time he was anxious, his bottom lip quivered. Like he was on the edge of sobbing like a baby. He pursed his lips to hide it. He couldn't lose any ground.

"I do have some of it. I even offered to show it to your boys, but they just laughed and walked away."

They glowered at him.

"Besides, wouldn't you rather get the whole chunk than a tiny piece of it? The day I pay you, it'll be the whole amount, and we'll be even. How's that sound?"

"What's going on, Alby?" said Barry from behind Ciro. "You okay, man?" He elbowed the goons out of the way.

"Who's this?" Ciro wanted to know. "Your girlfriend?"

"Who's asking?" Barry knew Ciro's reputation: a bully. He'd poke fun at the skinny kids, shove them around, and didn't care one way or another when the teachers threatened to send him to the principal's office.

"Ah, a live one." He let go of Alby and faced Barry. Ciro was a good two inches taller than Barry; even so, Alby saw that Barry didn't have to look up at Ciro. He stood eye to eye, and looked just as mean. Alby could let Barry go at it with Ciro right now, and that would take care of this little problem maybe. Or make it worse? Get his best friend into a big old bind?

When Barry didn't back away, even with the goons staring him down, Ciro said, "Girlfriend or no girlfriend, Alby, you come through, or else." He grabbed Alby's nose and twisted it.

Alby saw stars for a moment, then said, "Yeah, Ciro. Never mind my boy here. He's just looking out for me. Like your boys do for you. I'll take care of it. Don't you worry about that project, man."

"Project? Right. Sure." Whistling some silly tune, Ciro walked away with his gang of muscle, Barry glaring at them.

Alby shoved Barry. "Man, what's with you? Don't you know not to stick your nose into other people's business?"

Barry blinked. Hadn't he just saved Alby?

"That's right, Barry. Who do you figure you are, thinking you need to come in and rescue me? I can take care of myself." Of course, he was glad Barry had shown up when he did. Alby could have gotten another beating.

Pigheaded, Barry thought. *Whatever. Just walk away. For now.*

eight

Later, on the way to class from lunch, Barry had to know. "So, your mom said you had a project due. Was that it this morning with Ciro? What's going on?"

"What's going on? What's going on? I'll tell it to you straight, *again:* none of your beeswax is what's going on. You got me now?" Alby started walking away in a huff.

"Loud and clear."

Alby stopped. "We're good, then? Really, what gives you the right, Barry?"

"What'd you just say?" said Barry. He was standing still in the middle of the hall, looking straight into Alby's eyes. He wanted to see if there'd be the twinkle to show Alby was just kidding. Or the quivering lip that meant he was dead serious.

"That we're done talking about this, deal?" Alby looked away and felt his bottom lip begin to tremble.

"That's not what you said. You said, 'What gives you the right?'"

"Yeah, maybe. So? I mean, if you're not thinking of doing for me what I need, what I asked you nicely to do for a friend yesterday afternoon, then step back, or just plain out of the way, and let me do what I've got to do." He shifted, ready to walk.

"You know what, Alby? This morning I was going to tell you yes, that I'd fight like you'd asked. But now, forget it. Whatever your problem is with Ciro and the rest of his numb-nut tagalongs, it's all yours, like you said. If that's how you want it."

"It is," Alby said. But why'd he have to be that way—stubborn, prideful? Barry was telling him he'd get in the ring, come through for him like a true-blue friend, but Alby just had to have the final word. How easy it could've been to spill it. Come clean. Barry wouldn't let the cat out of the bag. Instead, Alby said, "Yeah, that's how it is."

"Fine by me." Barry began walking away, then turned: "Oh, and what gives me the right to dig my fat nose in your stupid business is the same thing that gave you the right to keep bugging me to come hang out with you after Pop died and I wasn't up for company. You kept it up day in, day out: 'Barry, let's go do this, let's go do that; get your mind off things for a while.' Remember?" Barry turned away and this time didn't look back. To himself he said, "It's called friendship, idiot."

nine

Here's how Barry remembered Alby's bugging him back then:

It'd been two weeks since Pop had passed. Most of that time, Barry stayed in the house. He went to school some days, some not, but he'd come straight home before Alby could catch up to him. At home, he didn't come out. Not to hang with Alby on the porch, hit the bags, mow the lawn, or go running.

One day, Alby showed up like he'd been doing every day after school. He knocked at the front door and asked Mrs. Esquivel, "Can Barry come out?"

"I don't think he will."

"Can I come in, then?" He didn't take no for an answer. First couple of times he stood outside Barry's door, knocked softly, and said, "Hey, Bare, I'm here to hang out and talk, or just hang out and shut up." No answer, so he knocked louder. "It's me, man. Alby. We don't have to do nothing if you don't want. It's just not good to be alone too much like you've been. Come on out." After a half hour, he said, "Well, I've got to eat something. Talk to you tomorrow," and went home.

The next couple of times, Alby knocked and knocked and knocked. He talked right through the door about what was happening at school. He jabbered away: "You know Rosa, from homeroom? Rumor is she's just broken up with Howard. How long have we been waiting for that?" No answer still. "Listen, what do you think if I put the moves on her? I know you kind of got the hots for her too, but we've signed no contract about matters like this one. Early bird, right? You'll be missing out." He kept up this nonsense, but nothing seemed to work.

The next week, they hung out at school over lunch, but he couldn't get Barry to talk. So they sat. A week later, Barry missed school, so Alby came over. He was about to knock when the door opened. "You're late," Barry said. "Usually you're here at four-thirty. What took you?"

"This," Alby said, showing him a hubcap for the Galaxie. "The fourth one. I been looking for it everywhere online. Found nothing but in sets of four, right? Folks just won't sell singles online. They say, 'If one's all you need, well, you don't break a set. You should know better.' Apparently these are collector's items. It's a crazy world, old cars. So I went to a couple of places Dad told me about. All those junkyards by the side of the expressway? Well, a few had tons of hubcaps hanging on walls, and willing to sell them as singles. There wasn't one for a Galaxie in the bunch. What they did have were all scratched up. I kept looking because I know you wouldn't settle for less than cherry. And good things come to those who wait, or whatever. So here."

He held it out. Barry seemed on the verge of tears, so before things got out of control, Alby turned and said, "I got the keys to the shop from your momma. You gonna help put this on, or am I doing it myself? The real question is, do you trust me to do it right?"

What Barry didn't know was that Alby not only went to a couple of yards looking for this part, he'd had to do more than just walk in and lo-and-behold there it was hanging all nice and clean on a wall. As a matter of fact, he got screamed at when he snapped one cap off a junker and carried it in. Most of the people working the counter said the same as the bozos online: "A set of four caps is a set of four. Not one, not two, not three. Four, got it?" What did it matter to Alby how many he bought? Plus it was cheaper to get them in town than online. Now he had the whole set. He toyed with the idea of giving them all, but for now, he decided to hand Barry the exact one he needed.

So Barry finally came out of his room, and the boys went into the shop. Alby could tell Barry was having a hard time, so he said, "Listen, man. You know what? Let me hang this one on the empty peg next to the others. I'll lock up. We can always do this another time. When you're good to go, you know."

A layer of dust covered everything, including Barry's punching bags.

Barry had nodded. He went outside, turned toward the house, and leaned on the wall of the shop. One leg was folded behind him, the sole of his shoe resting on the wood. He heard Alby clinking around inside and worried he'd mess something up, so he went in. Alby was standing over by the Peg-Board comparing his addition to the other three. "Mighty fine craftsmanship if I say so myself," he said. He polished the new hubcap on his sleeve. "Let's scoot."

"No," Barry said. "I'll tell you what, if you want to go, you can. I'm staying."

"Well, if you don't mind," said Alby, "then so will I."

"Cool."

"What are friends for, right, if not to hound you until you can't take it no more?"

The rest of the evening they dusted the place. All the while the Galaxie remained under the blue tarp just like Pop had left it.

It'd be a few more weeks before the cover came off and the hubcaps went on. That day, Barry said, "Man, Alby, Pop would've loved to see this."

Alby had wanted to say something like "From heaven, I think he does," but reconsidered because even though he really and truly meant it, a remark like that would sound corny. Silly. He kept his mouth shut.

But at least Barry was out and about, smiling some, talking. Even at school. Talking through his sadness. At least there was that.

ten

After school Alby looked for Barry over by the Coke machines where they usually met before walking home. He
wanted to say he was real sorry about turning his back this
morning, and for that crack about what right did he have to
stick his nose where it didn't belong. He'd stepped way over
the line.

Alby waited close to a half hour before deciding to
leave. *Maybe I shouldn't've told him to quit meddling in my life.*

Alby felt like a complete screwup.

He was halfway home now. He'd been thinking so hard
that he couldn't remember crossing Conway Avenue, and
now he was across the street from the little store on the
corner. He looked at the new truck outside. A sign on its
roof said, "Play the Lotto—Win a-Lotto More Than Just

Millions!" People were dumber than a stick to fall for that one. Using a shiny new truck to entice shoppers to buy lotto tickets; if their numbers hit, they'd win the jackpot and the truck. As if a winner of millions wouldn't already have it in his head to buy a new car of his own choosing. The store owners had rotated trucks several times already, without a single winning soul. But every time Alby stopped by, there was a line of dopes waiting to pay for a chance to win. "A fool's tax," Dad called it. "You don't see the wealthy wasting a dollar on those kinds of odds. If you're gonna toss money at something, chuck it at stocks, or even at cards, where there's a chance at some kind of a return."

Barry's momma never bought a ticket either. For her it had to do with saving up for new shoes for Barry, or for his college fund, or once a month, for a DVD rental and a pizza. Since they were kids, the two boys and Mrs. Esquivel had sat around the coffee table plenty of times watching some movie, laughing and stuffing their mouths.

After the movie one night, the winning lotto numbers were announced. "What I could do with seventeen million bucks!" Alby said.

Mrs. Esquivel smiled big at them and said, "I'm the richest woman in the world right now."

Look what good people they are. How could I doubt Barry? I'm going to tell him everything. We can deal with Ciro together. Tell him I was so wrong to say I didn't need his help. He has every right to expect to know my troubles. He'd also tell Barry he didn't have to fight in the Man o' Might competition.

They *would* mow lawns. Raise the cash that way. . . . Still, what a drag.

Last resort, he'd break down and ask Dad for some help but keep quiet about the reason. Beg if he had to. Barry was worth that much, and more.

He slapped his hands together: "That's the way to go."

Alby walked into the corner store happy. He wanted to cool off and get water for the rest of the trek. He saw Barry sitting at one of the booths, busy writing.

"Mind if I join you?" Alby asked.

Barry looked up. "Sure you can stoop so low?"

"Listen, Bare. About that—you don't know how sorry I am. You're my best friend. You got every right to jump in whenever, wherever you want to. Against whomever. Whether I want you to or not. Doesn't matter. You're out for my own good. And I was a jerk."

"Go on, fool." Barry smiled, motioning for Alby to sit.

Alby sat. "What you got there?"

"Well, I figured whatever it was bothering you, I have to do what I have to do, so I found out this is one of the places that's handing out applications for the Man o' Might fights." He shoved the paperwork over at Alby.

"I've changed my mind. I don't need you to do this for me. I'm thinking—"

"I've got my own reasons now, man. So sure, part of it is helping you out of whatever deep mess you've gotten yourself into, but Momma's a better reason. You should've seen how she looked this morning at breakfast. This is a no-brainer,

Alby. I win, everybody wins. I lose? Well, I just can't. So I've got to do this, and do it right. You with me?"

Alby nodded, but instead of feeling like an enormous burden had been lifted off him, his forty percent weighed him down in another way. Because it was money he'd be taking from the Esquivels. Right out of their pockets. He'd have to rethink those percentages. Times like this—his skin or Barry's?—hard as it seemed to choose, he'd take only what he needed to pay his debt.

"You with me?" Barry asked. "I still need that manager. I mean, if I'm going to be doing the sweating, I don't need to be filling out my own paperwork and worrying over my weight class and height and reach and do I have an in-the-ring nickname." Barry tried it out in his head: Barry "El Mero Mero" Esquivel. Nah—something about calling himself the Main Man just didn't ring true.

He tossed the pen to Alby, who said, "Sure, I'm in. I got your back, buddy. As for a nickname? We'll think of something." He thought of Barry the Bruiser or the Bone Cruncher. Nah. Barry wasn't ugly and nasty like that. But Best Bud or Big Old Teddy Bear wouldn't work, for obvious reasons.

Still, those names fit.

eleven

Later, on Momma's night off, she and Barry watched one of her favorite movies. She was all fidgety.

"You hungry?" he asked.

"No. Are you? You didn't get enough at dinner?"

"I did, but maybe before they're all gone I'll have some of those fingernails you keep eating away. With a little salt, some ketchup maybe."

Then she got it and slugged him on the shoulder. They laughed.

"Listen, Momma. I been thinking—and no, I didn't get a brain freeze, and it didn't hurt so much."

She smiled. "What about, mi'jo?"

"Well, when something like this comes up, I mean something serious, I ask myself, 'Barry, what would Pop do in this situation?' Then I hear Pop clear as day share with me some of his worldly wisdom, those pearls of his, remember?"

She relaxed into the couch and smiled, remembering. "Sure, always something from the Bible, or a silly story about boxing, then that big grin of his. So, what's he telling you?"

"He says, 'Mi'jo, you do what you have to to take care of your momma right.'"

"What are you planning? You can only mow so many lawns. Besides, I'll get a better job soon. I've started looking." She pointed to the want ads on the coffee table. "But if things don't start looking up, you could sell—" She stopped.

"Sell what?"

"Nothing. Never mind."

The Galaxie. "You may be on to something, Momma. It's a beaut—Pop's and my baby—but he'd sell it for a dime if it would get us out of a jam. Don't worry about selling just yet. I got other plans for now."

She seemed relieved.

Sure, life would get a little tight for a bit, but they'd lived on pasta and sauce, toasted bread, and Kool-Aid before. The Galaxie was worth thinking about, but later. Right now, the Man o' Might would be the plan. But he wanted her permission first.

"Something else Pop tells me: 'She's working too hard. Cut your momma whatever break you can, mi'jo.' So, here's my plan. Me and Alby—"

"Ai, ai, ai," she said, smiling and shaking her head. "Now I know it's trouble if Alby's in on this. But go on."

"No, this is a good plan. You know Pop made sure I could take care of myself in every which way, including boxing. Trained two hours almost every night here or at the gym. Now, before you get all scrunched up in the face, Momma, hear me out. You know I'm good at boxing. I know how you feel about it, that it's a terrible, horrible thing, that I might get hurt."

"Absolutely right. Two men beating on each other, and the object's to clean the other guy's clock. Where's the sport in that? And I still haven't changed my mind."

"You might just have to, at least this once, Momma. Besides, you know I'm good, right? Why else have I been training so hard for so long? I'm real good."

"Yes, mi'jo, you're good, but—"

Barry cut her off with a palm up and a quick shake of his head. "There's this event downtown this weekend. It's . . . this sort of competition you're not too keen on. But there's also a cash prize. I don't know how much exactly, but Alby says it could be seven hundred fifty bucks, mas o menos. And whatever I win, my percentage, well, it goes into paying off some bills. What do you say?"

"No. Under no circumstances; no, no, no. I won't have my son going around fighting for money. No."

"Momma, I'm going to do this." *For money*—the idea was a shot to his gut. *That's why Pop left Fabian. But this is different. Right?* "I'm asking permission. I won't do it if you tell me no for real. But how am I supposed to feel when I've got an opportunity knocking real loud and I can't answer it? I don't like seeing you worried and dead tired. I don't need to see you working like this, and all for what? Me, my college fund, and me again. It's not right to pass up this chance. I won't. And you know Pop wouldn't have either."

Pop probably would not have let him do it: "Mi'jo, this kind of fighting's not real; it's not sanctioned." Barry shook Pop's voice from his head.

Another movie started. He took a different approach. "We're hard up. The bills aren't disappearing."

Momma stared at the TV and crossed her arms.

"Let me do my part."

Two hours later, after the movie ended, she said, "Do it if you think you have to. I can't tell you what not to do anymore. You're a grown man. But two things you need to know: I'm looking for another job, and thanks for thinking like this." She leaned over and kissed him on the cheek. "Oh, three things, okay four: whatever way Alby's involved, make sure he doesn't take advantage of you; and last, if you decide to go through with this, don't think I'm going to see you get beat on."

"As if," he said. But one thing he realized: things must've been worse than he thought, because she didn't absolutely, outright, without a doubt, no way no how forbid it.

He just had to win.

twelve

Next day after school, Alby set out for downtown Mission, where the Man o' Might would take place in what used to be a dress shop. He was on foot because Dad had taken away his driving privileges about a month ago; he'd accidentally dented the bumper on a date. Alby was okay with that. He wouldn't have to walk everywhere forever.

A block from the place, Alby could see a couple of guys putting up half sheets of plywood on the windows just high enough so light could still come in but no one could peek without paying. The wood was warped and coming apart at some of the corners, like mice had eaten through.

"Say," he said when he was close enough.

Neither of the guys turned, so he stood right next to one of them: "Say, can you give me some help?"

The worker didn't look at Alby. "Does it look like I can just drop what I'm doing to give you a hand?" he said through scrunched-up lips, chomping down on a few nails.

"I'm just looking for where to sign up for the Man o' Might, man. Didn't mean to tear you away from this important work." Alby'd learned early on from both Mom and Dad that when you want something done right "you have to put a guy in his place from the get-go to get where you want to go." That was one of Mom's sayings. And if it meant being rude, so be it.

"Whatever you say, kid. Go around back, in the door says Exit, ask for Mike. He'll take good care of you."

Alby moved in that direction, then turned when the man said: "Yo, kid. The registration fee's not much, but it's a foregone conclusion you're gonna lose the fifteen bucks. So why don't you do this for me? Just slip me three five-spots right now, avoid getting hurt, and be done with it." He laughed.

Alby walked away.

"Get a load of this skinny-bones punk, Joe. He's the best this place's got to offer, I guess. Easy pickings. We got another one in the bag."

"Yeah," said Joe. "I wonder what other action we can find if that's the case?"

But Alby was gone. *Who cares what those chumps say? They can think whatever they want. What they don't know will come back and bite them, hard.* He chuckled and turned the corner into the alley.

He found Mike sitting behind a folding table in front of a gray cash box. He was stocky, like he lifted weights. Behind him, some guys were putting the ring together. Mike was on a cell phone: "Yeah, yeah. I got you," he said. He motioned for Alby to wait. "It's too late for that." He made a face at Alby, meaning the guy on the other end was being a jerk. "Call me later. I got somebody here." He closed the phone. "What can I do for you?"

"Well, I need to turn in my fighter's application. They tell me Mike's the man in charge."

Mike smiled at that. "I'm your guy. What you got for me?" He stretched out his hand.

"Before I hand this in," Alby said, flicking a finger at his paper, "I got a few questions."

"Sure, my friend. Knock yourself out." He laughed. "Get it?" He made like he was shadowboxing. "A little fighting humor." He picked up a Gatorade, took a swig, then wiped his mouth. "This Rio Grande Valley of yours, it's hot. So what can I do you for?"

"First, about the registration fee of fifteen dollars—what kind of help can you offer me on that score?"

"How do you mean?"

"Well, an operation like you've got going here, I figure you're about getting cash in hand as quick as you can to cover the overhead. It only makes sense—like my dad has told me countless times, in business the important thing is you got money coming in. 'The sticker price isn't a fixed thing,' the old man tells me. 'Deals are for making.' So what

I mean is this: I *got* the fifteen bucks on me, but can you do better for me? I mean, look at that." He pointed at the stack of applications. "Thirty, forty apps? It doesn't look like you're hurting."

"Closer to fifty, but whatever. Let me get this right: you want me to cut you a better deal? And why would I want to do that?" Mike leaned back in his squeaky chair, snapping the fingers of one hand.

Alby could see it in Mike's face: he'd get a deal. He'd counter with ten, and Mike would go down to thirteen, and they'd settle on eleven or twelve.

"First," he said, pointing at the applications, "a few bucks short here or there isn't going to break you. Second, I got a boy I'm signing up who's going all the way. I'm not talking he stands a fair chance. I'm not saying you'll be on the edge of your seat thinking maybe he will, maybe he won't. I'm saying, without a doubt, my boy'll take it all. You can bet every penny of these fees you're charging, and you'll come out richer by whatever odds are on the table. Assuming there'd be a bit of that kind of action on the side, which I'm sure there won't be." He knew he was talking nonsense now, but Alby'd come across Mike's type before at school and at Dad's car lot—the guy saw an easy way to make some dough, and he'd take it. Alby had to admit he was that type too. But not so sleazy as Mike.

When he mentioned "action on the side," a sparkle lit up Mike's eyes. He knew Alby was talking about betting on the side, which was illegal but happened all the time. Guys gathered in some corner and wanted to know how much you wanted to bet, on what fighter, and what odds you'd take: two-to-one odds meant he'd make two bucks for every dollar he put on the line. What if someone was crazy enough to give him five to one, or ten to one? He could make a killing! After a fight, these same guys would come together and money changed hands. It was that easy.

Mike leaned forward and rubbed his nose. "I don't know about that. This is a legitimate game we're running here. Gambling, well, we both know the laws in Texas. We don't condone anything of that nature. What folks in the audience do on their own, that's their business. My end's all on the up-and-up. Fifteen dollars for the registration, ten at the door. Thirty percent of concessions. I may not be getting rich off this, but it's a living. You know what I'm saying?"

Something told Alby this guy was trying too hard. What was it Shakespeare said? "Methinks the lad protests too much," or something like that.

"And about this fighter of yours going all the way, I seen some tough guys already come in, and they paid the whole fifteen. What's different about your boy? Why shouldn't he pay up like everybody else?"

"Easy—he's got a manager like me who worries over the details. A manager who knows the racket. Those other guys, they're amateurs. So what do you say?"

"Ah, kid, you're a born hustler. You talked me into it. How about ten?"

"I was thinking maybe five, but ten's good." He didn't

have to, but Alby paid Mike with a twenty. He wanted to make an impression: it wasn't that he was hurting for cash, he wasn't begging for handouts. No way—he was his own man, and nobody should mistake him for a sap. He was a real wheeler-dealer.

He handed over the application. Mike studied it, flipped it over. "Your boy? Barry—he's eighteen, right? Got to be eighteen or older. What's Barry's DOB? The eleventh of this month, huh?"

"Yeah, sure, the eleventh." What a putz he was. He'd just forgotten Barry's birthday. Again. And how come Barry had kept quiet about it? Too embarrassed there'd be no party? He'd probably mowed a couple of lawns in celebration. Alby felt awful, but he'd make it up to Barry somehow.

"I mean, if he had to, and I'm not saying he has to, but if the authorities came snooping around like they do, could he show ID that says so?"

Alby pressed his lips together, did a funky thing with his shoulders, and nodded once. Why was this guy pressing him about Barry's age? "Tell you what. I'll have Barry bring his driver's license Saturday as proof. How's that?"

Maybe after he'd take Barry out for some ice cream or a burger. He'd pay out of his forty percent. Yeah, he was already thinking like a winner, looking ahead to the postfight celebrations.

He forgot he'd been considering giving Barry a bigger cut, if not all of the winnings.

"Here's how this competition works," said Mike. "Your

fighter will be assigned a time slot and an opponent. If he wins, he moves on. If not, then he's out. If your boy's as good as you say he is, he just might make it to the Fence o' Fighting match. If he does, then he goes into the ring to fight an as-yet-unannounced former pro. Fights'll last three rounds, one minute each. You still up to it?"

"So there's an actual fence around the ring for that match?"

"Sure. But it's mostly for show. You haven't filled in the blank for a nickname. I got a list you can pick from." Mike handed Alby a half sheet of paper.

Alby looked at the top and wanted to laugh: "A-Bombastic," "The Absolute Package," "The Agitator," and "The Assassin." "When do you need to know?"

"Is this your number on the app?"

Alby nodded.

"Tell me his nickname when I call you to tell you what time your boy's match is at. Oh, and take this—look it over for him, and have him sign it. It's for insurance purposes. Not that anything'll go wrong, but business is business. And you know about that. Do me a favor; tell him happy belated for me."

Alby smiled. "Sure thing." He took the paper. "One more thing, Mike. What's the purse?"

"Purse? Like you said, I got overhead to worry about first. That's a good amount: rent on the place, the bleachers and ringside chairs, advertising, labor. And what if every fighter had a manager who wanted to cut deals on the registration?

It all depends. I'll know more later," he said, and put the application on the stack, then grabbed his phone and began dialing.

"Cool," Alby said. "I'll talk at you later."

He sauntered down the middle of the sidewalk to the next corner in case the two schmucks putting up plywood were eyeballing him. He stopped and glanced over his shoulder. They were still covering up the windows. So he sat on the curb.

He wished he'd gotten Mike to nail down an amount so he could tell Barry. "It depends" wouldn't go over well. But he'd tell Barry about the number of applications, and tomorrow he'd ask Mike when he called. Maybe later go online and Google it. Right now, he felt good and light. He took a deep breath and smiled. Things were looking up.

And maybe if he had to, just to guarantee making more than enough to pay his debt, and for Barry to be able to hand over a bigger wad of cash to his momma, Alby'd place a bet here and there himself. *What could it hurt?*

thirteen

That night, Barry sat in the living room watching the news. Momma was at work. He'd fixed himself some leftovers and was about done when he heard Alby at the front door.

"Hey, Bare."

"Come in. Just watching the weather."

The screen door squeaked open and shut. "I got something for you. Three things, actually. One's to sign. Insurance papers. A sort of just-in-case. Routine; everybody's got to be on file." He handed Barry the paper.

Barry took it. He hadn't thought he could get seriously hurt. He'd read on a Web site at school today about a guy winning a similar fight in England, and a day or two later he was dead. But the doctors couldn't be sure if it had to do with the fighting. And besides, that other event was more like street fighting, no-holds-barred. The Man o' Might was boxing. The fine print on the flyer said headgear mandatory, and they'd be using fourteen-ounce gloves. That meant padding.

"Just routine," Alby said.

Barry read it over, noticed all kinds of misspelled words, and grammar and punctuation errors. *Will this even hold up in court?* he wondered. But he'd sign it anyhow. *Really, what can go wrong? A couple bruised ribs? A black eye?* He'd been hurt more playing tackle football in the neighborhood. *Worst maybe a broken nose?* "Sure, hoops we got to jump through," he said, and went for a pen in the kitchen drawer.

Good, thought Alby. "Besides, all the others better sign that form in triplicate before they get in the ring with you. Does it say anything on there about what ER they'll be taken to after?" He laughed.

Barry came back into the living room, where Alby was eating the last of the potato chips on Barry's plate. "You said you have three things to show me?"

"Oh, this," Alby said, and handed Barry a box tied with colored string. "You got some soda to wash this down?"

"In the fridge. What's this?"

"Open it. Find out."

"Sure, and since you're up, get me a soda too."

"Heh. Listen to you. The big shot now that you're in the fights. Sign on a couple of dotted lines, and you're ordering everybody around like you're the king of the ring. Well, I'll tell you what," Alby said, looking serious, his lip quivering just a tiny bit. He'd have to work on that more. "As your manager, tell me this one thing: ice or no ice?" He left for the kitchen.

As soon as Alby was gone, Barry undid the string, opened the box, and pulled out a silver pen. It was inscribed "Champ." "Thanks."

"Don't sweat it; it's from your fridge."

"No, I mean the pen. What's it for?"

"Oh, yeah. You like it? Mom drove me to the mall for it. Happy belated birthday. You didn't think I forgot, did you?" It had cost him twenty bucks, but it had been worth it, even if it had come out of his stash; so had the registration fee.

"Nope." They were quiet, then Barry said, "So, are we set, then?"

"Pretty much. I'm waiting for a call from this guy Mike, the promoter. He said he'd let me know when your first fight was. And how much the prize's going to be too."

They sat quietly, staring at the TV. "So he didn't even hint at how much?" Barry asked. "I mean, I'm counting on it being enough. Told Momma five hundred, seven fifty, give or take."

"Said he'd know more tomorrow. But it's got to be a good bit. I've been reading up on it. Never a prize less than seven hundred fifty bucks. He must've had fifty applications at fifteen bucks a pop. Plus ticket sales and concessions, he said. You do the math."

"Okay, I guess."

They sat through some stupid infomercial about losing

your love handles and replacing them with tight, cut abs. Alby joked, "My stomach's a solid piece of workmanship. Yours, on the other hand, is nothing but flab." He reached over and poked Barry's gut. "You got to work that off, bud. How do you expect to win on Saturday with blubber like that slowing you down?"

They both laughed.

"Oh, third thing. We have to come up with a nickname. Check these out."

Barry took the list and began laughing. "Velvet Elvis? WMD? Your Daddy? Where do they get this stuff?"

"You're telling me. The whole list is like that," said Alby. "We don't have to come up with one now, but by tomorrow maybe." He got up from the couch. "Hey, I got to go. Wait on that phone call. I'll let you know your schedule tomorrow at school." He folded up the signed paper, stuffed it in his shirt pocket. "Knock on wood—maybe it'll be even more than seven hundred and fifty dollars. It just came to me: how about Barry the Bear? Tough, huh? Think it over. Later, then."

The Bear, Barry thought. *It works. And that's a lot of money.* When he'd signed that insurance form, it hit Barry: he was in this deep already. Nothing said he couldn't pull out, but he'd signed two papers now that said he'd go through with it. Momma and Alby were counting on him now.

He wasn't scared to get in the ring. He knew he was good. Nothing bad would happen. Not really.

But what if he lost?

fourteen

At school on Friday, everybody stepped out of Barry's way in the halls, looked at him from afar, whispered in each other's ears. Word about him fighting had got out. Did his teachers and the principal know? If they did, would they confront him, try and talk some sense into him? What would he say?

What did it matter anyway? Barry had to fight. This morning Momma had looked tired. Barry knew it was something else bothering her. So he asked.

Momma looked up finally and said, "It's just, well, here," she said, and passed him an envelope. It was the payment on the house for fifty dollars more per month. A note from the mortgage company said the increase was due to a reassessment of property in the county. On paper, the Esquivels' home was now worth a good deal more than they had bought it for, and so more had to be put in the escrow account to pay taxes and insurance.

"It's going to be okay, Momma." *Can things get any worse?* he'd thought.

So now, he didn't want any of this silly attention at school.

Meanwhile, Alby was digging it. Already he'd lined up a date with one of the pretty cheerleaders, had gotten patted on the back by some of the jocks, who all wished him and Barry luck. Even Ciro and his goons kept clear. Win-win all the way around for him.

What was more important to Alby, though, was that Barry was quiet, like he didn't want to talk, which was good news, because besides finding out that Barry's first bout was going to be at nine-thirty a.m., he'd also found out the purse was a hundred bucks and some other prizes. A big fat nada. *So what kind of people do this sort of thing for just a hundred?* Alby wondered. *Fools like the ones buying lotto tickets for a chance to win big. Why else?* He and Barry weren't fools like that. They each had a real reason.

What if he told Barry about the purse and Barry decided not to fight? It only made sense. Why would he want to get in the ring one match after another if he'd be getting paid close to squat—sixty percent of squat? He'd pull out. *But if I keep it to myself, I'll see about placing a bet or two. I'm bound to make some dough on the first two or three matches.* Bet heavy and hard early on, because nobody but Alby knew who this Barry kid was and what Barry had in him. How many times had Alby seen him go at that heavy bag? The others were clueless, and what man wouldn't want to bet on his own fighter against a young, unknown, pimply-faced schoolkid? They'd be idiots not to take whatever odds Alby was laying then. That'd be the time to make the real bucks, before people saw that Barry could win. Would anyone be dumb enough to take three-to-one odds? Alby imagined how much he could make. For every buck he put up, he'd win three. Easy money.

For now, he'd zip his lips. As manager, he'd be doing his fighter a favor: *I mean, why even worry Barry with this sort of news if chances are still very good we'll make a killing? I've just got to play my cards right.*

He leaned into Barry. "They love you, man. They're all rooting for you. Can you feel the positive energy they're beaming at you? I can." He put his arm around Barry's shoulders.

"Yeah, sure."

"Hey," said Alby. Was Barry getting the prefight jitters? Was the pressure too much? Alby wasn't sure he wanted to know. Instead of asking, "Hey, Bare, what's going on?" he said, "Hey, Bare, what's with the dopey look? Champions aren't ever all down in the face in public. They look, well, like champions, which you are, my friend."

Barry tried to smile. He considered telling Alby about the extra house payment every month, but he didn't want to sound like a crybaby. "Just putting on the game face, Alby."

In the lunchroom the principal walked right by his table with not even a nod in his direction, and all through the school day not one teacher approached Barry about the fights. Last period, all Barry did was stare at the clock. The bell rang.

He was scot-free.

fifteen

That night Barry sat at the kitchen table writing a note for Momma to read after he'd left for the fights in the morning. He tried his best to reassure her: "And if it comes down to it," he wrote, "there's always the Galaxie. I mean, this was part of Pop's and my plan, and how many times has Coach Pelfrey offered to buy it from us? And for good money too."

He put down the pen. Coach had offered them $12,500. That would help. But was Barry willing to let go of the car so easily? The car he and Pop had worked on? *As much as you loved it, Pop, you'd say, "Mi'jo, big picture, that Galaxie, pretty as it is, isn't nothing more than a bucket of bolts. A big old doorstop if you don't put it to use. Do what you've got to do."*

After the fights, he'd take a part-time job at the Dairy Queen or wait tables at Taco Olé. In the summer after graduation, he'd go full-time wherever he was working and look for a part-time gig somewhere else. Keep doing lawns. He was young, he had the energy. He was the man of the house. It was his responsibility. Momma would say she didn't want him throwing away his future, that it was her job to take care of her boy no matter how old he was, no matter if he was growing a mustache or driving his own car, he was still her babychild, and that was that. "There's no, no, no way," she would say, "I'm going to let you throw your college away. We'll get by, mi'jo. You make sure you keep your grades up for those scholarships."

And he'd hold her hand across the table and say, "All fine and good, Momma, but get it out of your head that if I take a job or two I'm sacrificing my education. That university isn't going nowhere. So let me do this; besides, like Pop used to say, 'God helps those who help themselves.'" He'd grip her hand tighter and smile at her. "For sure, I'll start school next summer at the latest. But right now, it's time for me to work."

Then he heard Alby at the door. "Come on in," he said. "What's up?"

"Not much. Just checking in on my fighter. Wondering if you needed anything."

Yeah, a cool 100K would do the trick. "Nope. Just came in from hitting the bag."

"Good. That's real good, but don't overdo it."

"Nah. Going to bed. I want to be good and rested for tomorrow."

Alby toyed with the idea of coming clean about the purse, saying how if he wanted to, Barry should pull out now, no big loss. They'd do something else to raise money.

"How about you, Alby? You need anything?" Barry asked.

"Like you. I'm right as rain. You need your rest, so I better scoot on out of here. One thing."

"What's that?"

"No, never mind."

"What? What?"

"Well, I was thinking about, maybe— No, nothing. I'll figure it out myself. It's nothing, really." Alby knew what Barry would say about them laying some bets; he'd say, "Alby, that kind of money is worthless, not earned, plain wrong." So Alby would keep his mouth shut. *Bare never has to know. Let him think it was the winnings.* "Fight's at nine-thirty. What time should I be here to pick you up? Dad's letting me drive the car tomorrow. Told him I had something special lined up and needed to drive to arrive in style. How cool is that?"

"Cool enough, I guess. I want to take a morning warm-up run around seven to be out of the house before Momma's awake. I'll meet you at your house around eight. Get there early to scope out the place."

They were quiet.

"Alby?"

"Yeah?"

"Barry 'The Bear' Esquivel—it's got a certain ring to it, don't you think?"

Alby smiled. "Glad you like it. That's what I told the guy when he called. I'll see you later, then."

Alby left, relieved Barry hadn't brought up the rest of Alby's conversation with Mike. Walking across the back-yard, he thought, *I did the right thing. But still . . .*

Looking at Alby walking away, Barry rubbed the knot in his stomach. It'd been there since morning. Nothing he did helped.

sixteen

"I got that, Bare," Alby said. He took Barry's bag from the backseat. They walked into the makeshift arena in silence. People were just beginning to arrive. Most of the men looked older, and mean, despite their loud laughing.

Barry reached for the handle, but Alby beat him to it. "Today, bud, you're the man. I can't have you spending any energy on the little things." They pushed through a heavy canvas curtain and found themselves in the dressing room. There were already a few fighters there.

Barry looked to his right and saw a guy sprawled out on a bench. Somebody was waving smelling salts under his nose. The guy groaned and yanked his head away from the stinging ammonia. He got up on an elbow, shook his head, then dry-heaved over a bucket.

"One down," Alby said. He grabbed Barry by the elbow and said, "Over there, Bare." He pointed to a bench at the other end of the room. He put Barry's bag down. "I'm going to see what I can see. You sit here. Relax."

"Easy for you to say," said Barry. He glanced over at the guy still heaving.

"Aw, him? Don't worry about him. He's not you. And you? You're the champ." Alby stepped away, then turned around: "I'll come get you when it's time, okay?"

"Sure. I'll be right here."

Barry was excited and nervous at the same time. Today wasn't going to lead to the Olympics or much else, but it would be his first fight in a real ring facing someone who'd be firing back. Barry looked at the guy on the bench. He was sitting up, but he was pale, like he was about to fall asleep. *What if . . . ?* He rubbed his forehead, hoping to wipe away the doubt. *Don't lose before you even get out there. Remember what Pop used to say: "Don't get caught with anything, including thinking like a loser."*

He took out a couple of rolls of tape and gauze, his gloves, his headgear, a mouthpiece, his trunks and a muscle shirt, and his shoes. He put on the shoes, tying the laces tight. He flexed his feet and rotated his ankles. Did a couple of squats, trying to get the right feel to the shoes. Then he wrapped some tape around the laces. He changed into his trunks, then tucked in the muscle shirt. He would've liked Alby to help tape up his fists, but he'd been doing this on his own for close to a year now. *Man, the way Pop used to do it, it felt like the tape wasn't even there*, he thought. He wished Pop was here. Earlier that morning, he'd felt nervous, so before heading to meet Alby, he sat in the driver's seat of the Galaxie, gripping the steering wheel. The quiet helped calm him. He saw the minigloves dangling from the rearview mirror, smiled, and took them. He grabbed his bag and sprinted up and down the street to warm up.

In the dressing room, waiting for Alby to come back, Barry reached into his bag and pulled the gloves out. He thought back to when Pop had gotten them. On the drive back from South Carolina, Pop talked nonstop about how they'd fix up the car, and when they were done, if Barry wanted, he could drive it to the prom. "If you can get a date, that is," Pop joked. Barry punched him lightly on the shoulder. "Is that all you've got?" Pop asked. Then he laughed. "It's all about technique, mi'jo. You've got to know it up here and in here," he said, pointing at his head and chest. "If you do, there's no stopping you."

Holding the little gloves right now, Barry said a quick prayer and put them back in the bag. He took a roll of gauze and started on his left hand. A few times around the wrist. Next he worked his way up, front and back, leaving his thumb uncovered, then all the way to the knuckles. He used up the rest of the roll on the knuckles. Then did it all again with the tape. When he was done, he punched his other palm a few times. It felt good, so he moved on to the right hand.

He opened and clenched his fingers around the tape

now. Getting the blood circulating. Pop had once said, "In a real match, the ref'll check that you didn't sneak a little extra something into your tape. He'll sign his name on the back of your taped hands or wrists then. Just in case. Some fighters or trainers, mi'jo, they'll go to any lengths to get what they want." Would this ref check his wrappings? To be safe, he left the gloves off.

"Good," Alby said, "you're dressed. You're on in twenty, so do whatever you need to get ready."

This morning's run had gotten the heat flowing. Now he made like he was jumping rope to warm up. The ref hadn't come to check on him, so he had Alby lace up the gloves. "Good and tight now." Then he did some quick stretching of the legs and back, shadowboxed, dipped left and right like he did with the big bag, and loosened his shoulders and neck. "Ready when you are."

"That's what I like to hear," Alby said.

※

Brawlin' Billy Martinez looked buff from across the ring. The ref called them to the middle of the mat and announced the fighters. Up close, Billy was the real deal, the veins on his biceps bulging, his clenching and unclenching fists working his forearms into a muscle frenzy. His face was leathery and tan-stretched. He looked about twenty. Five eight and 180 pounds. Barry was five ten and weighed 165. *Not going to be easy,* he thought, and remembered the fighter lying on the bench back in the dressing room. *Stop it,* he told himself. *Don't think like that!*

Next, the ref gave the two boxers his instructions: "Fellas, I want a good clean fight. Keep your blows above the waist; even with the gear, try not to knock heads; you're fighting three one-minute rounds; and if, for whatever reason, you can't go on no more, it's better you let me know. No shame in that. Now shake hands and back to your corners."

Brawlin' Billy grunted at Barry and shoved him at the shoulder. "I own you." Barry chomped down on his mouthpiece and adjusted his headgear.

Back in his corner, Barry was uneasy; he hoped it didn't show on his face or in his shifting from foot to foot.

Alby whispered, "Did the ref call him *Bawlin'* Billy?" He laughed.

Barry tried to smile. The bell rang, the fighters charged to the center of the ring. Barry felt good. In shape. For the first few seconds, they sized each other up. A jab here, a hook there. Brawlin' Billy liked to fight head-on. He jabbed two or three times with his left, then went for the big, reckless haymaker, a wild punch, usually overhead and telegraphed, meant to knock Barry out. But Billy kept missing.

Barry caught most of the jabs with his gloves and forearms and kept safely out of range of the whoppers. He shot a few jabs of his own, straight shots to the face, ribs, and gut. He occasionally threw a hook to the liver.

The bell sounded to end the first round. Alby jumped into the ring and said, "What you doing out there, Bare?

You're letting this cat eat you up. Take care of it. Of him. And now."

Barry took a small swig of water, spit it out, and said, "What are you talking about? I got it. Don't worry." What would Pop have told him about his first-ever round? Maybe "Stay on your game, mi'jo. You're headed for a win, but it isn't over yet."

The second round was much of the same, except that Barry's straight left to the sternum followed by a hook to the liver combination was finding its mark. Billy started grabbing hold of Barry, leaning every one of his 180 pounds on Barry's shoulders and neck. Barry had to dance his way.

Halfway into the third round, Billy was breathing heavy and Barry caught him with a right uppercut to the jaw, then a jarring left hook to his temple. Billy collapsed onto the mat and the ref counted to ten. Barry had won his first bout by kayo—a knockout! He was 1–0. He pumped a fist up to the sky. "Yeah!"

Alby climbed into the ring and held Barry's arm up in victory. The crowd was out of its seats screaming, happy they'd seen a knockout. That was what they'd come for. The place was almost filled.

Alby pulled Barry over to Mike, who was about to announce the winner. Alby said, "Didn't I tell you, Mike? My boy's got the goods." He looked at Billy sitting dazed in his corner, getting the salts to his nose. "*Brawlin'* Billy? More like *Sprawlin'* Billy."

Mike laughed. "Ladies and gentlemen," he said, "in the

losing corner, *Sprawlin'* Billy Martinez. And the winner by knockout, Barry 'The Bear' Esquivel. Put your hands together. Wasn't that an awesome battle?" Everyone was cheering and clapping. Then the ref was announcing the next match. Barry and Alby left for the locker room.

Up the aisle, people called to him and held out their hands for him to high-five them. "What you got in those gloves, boy? Rocks?" They slapped him on the back.

Barry couldn't help smiling at hearing his name. *Pop would've loved it*.

"That Billy had no game," Alby said.

Barry shook his head. "He was good, Alby. Better than you think."

"Maybe, but you knocked him out. Didn't I tell you this was a good idea?"

He flung an arm around Alby's neck. "Awesome!" he said. Barry had won his first fight by knockout.

In the locker room some fighters came over to Barry and congratulated him. He was happy, but he just nodded at them, thinking, *This is how Fabian would've acted after winning*. The rest of the time, Barry kept a scowl on his face like Fabian in the postcard.

Alby said, "You rest up, bud. I'm going to scout out the competition. Be back later." He went straight for the concession stands, where men were gathering to pay out, collect, and bet some more. Not knowing what to expect from Barry, Alby hadn't looked for saps willing to take any bets like he'd planned. So he took up only a hundred twenty-five. He could stop now but there was Ciro to worry about, and maybe Barry wouldn't appreciate doing all this work for a measly hundred bucks. And if he lost, then they wouldn't even have that.

Besides, now guys who wanted a chance at getting their money back agreed to what Alby was offering on Barry's next fight: "Three to one, my guy wins. How about we start at five dollars for the slowpokes, move to ten, then fifteen if there's any takers." These guys looked hungry for money. A few of them, Alby swore, might've been carrying guns stuck in their waists. Knives for sure.

Barry's next two fighters didn't even last the first round. These guys were older than Brawlin' Billy, and out of shape. Big, but slow and heavy. Not used to going a hundred and ten percent, using every part of their body to hit and keep from getting hit. At first they played to the audience, waving their arms as they ran around the ring, the crowd cheering them on. Next, they danced around Barry, but on a bob-in Barry caught each one hard on the side of the head. Each guy went down on a knee.

One took the eight count before managing to get back up on wobbly legs. A few moments later, Barry shot a vicious body blow that sent the guy stumbling back into the ropes, where he hung on even after the ref ordered him to come out to the middle of the ring and box. The ref waved his arms over his head and called it: "It's over."

The other fighter staggered over to his corner and sat

on the canvas. He kept staring at Barry. The saddest look on his face.

After each match, Alby escorted his fighter to the locker room behind the bleachers, and Barry heard the buzz: "Who is this kid? Is he the real deal? Someone we can count on?"

What were they counting on him for? He was here to win, whatever the payout would be. Alby'd told him, "Hey, buddy, you worry about the man in front of you. I'll worry about the prize." Alby looked kind of distracted, but Barry's only concern was not to let the other man get the jump on him. That was what Pop would've said.

He was 3–0. If it kept going like this, he'd be in the final match after two more fights. *Win that match and win the big money. And I'll be the champ!*

Alby said, "I'll be right back. But if they call your name and I'm not here, go right ahead without me." Alby had now made enough to pay Ciro off, with maybe fifty dollars left over. How could he hand Barry fifty bucks! *I've got to do better than that.*

Barry was tempted to poke his head out of the locker room and check out the competition, but he sat and rested instead.

✳

"And in this corner, Barry 'The Bear' Esquivel," the ref announced for the fourth time, and everyone cheered: "Go,

Bear! Go, Bear!" Barry tried to take it in stride, but it was his name they were calling. *Man, this is so cool!* He raised a glove to them.

On the way up to the ring, he saw Alby over by the concession stand with Ciro and his hoods. Ciro was rubbing his chin, his lips pursed. He looked over at Barry and their eyes met. He shook hands with Alby, who walked away fast to meet Barry.

"What was that about, Alby? What's Ciro want with you here? What did you hand him?"

"Right now, bud, it's this heavy across the ring you want to worry about. My thing was just some old business I had to take care of." Alby scanned the crowd over his shoulder, then turned back to Barry. "Now look, beat this guy and the next one, then you'll be in the Fence. We absolutely got to win that one. Otherwise, it's all been for nothing." He rubbed Barry's shoulders.

He shook Alby off. "Sure, whatever. But you better not be doing anything stupid."

The ref called the two fighters to the center of the ring, and as Barry heard his instructions, he thought, *What's Alby up to?*

Tito "The Titan" Gomez lasted all of forty-seven seconds into the second round before his girlfriend manager threw in the towel. He couldn't catch his breath, and knots were forming around the edges of his eyes.

Alby was missing again. Without waiting for Mike's announcement, Barry left the ring and went in search of Ciro.

He'd get to the bottom of Alby's business one way or another.

He couldn't find Ciro, so he went to the locker room to rest, put a bag of ice on his right cheekbone, another one on his left shoulder, and sat down to give his back and legs some kind of break. He wasn't out of juice yet, but one fight after another with less and less time between matches was taking its toll. Barry took a deep breath and hoped Alby would show. *Some manager.*

After Barry's fight with Brawlin' Billy, the locker room had been full of men, gym bags, and nervous chatter. Now Barry saw he was the only one there. Except for one bag, the place was empty. *Must be my guy's.*

Mike came in. He had a gym bag with him and sat at a bench in the far corner. Barry went up to him. "Hey, man, how's it going?"

"Good," Mike answered. "How's it with you? You left the ring quick; I thought you were hurt or something."

"Nah, just trying to take it easy."

"You're a natural. That's not a bad-looking uppercut you got. Good hook, too. One more to go and you'll be in the Fence. You tired?"

"Nah. I'll make it okay. But I wonder, Alby, my manager, he hasn't told me nothing about how much the prize will be. What'll be our take-home if I win?"

"He hasn't told you? I gave him all the details over the phone. The prize is a hundred dollars, some other stuff, too. For a start-up venture like mine, I'll be lucky to break even.

I'm left with just enough to go on to the next town, the next fight. I can't believe he didn't explain all this to you earlier. Some manager."

Some friend.

Mike must've seen his shock because he tried to sound upbeat: "Hey, but a hundred's a hundred, and I hear your buddy's getting some good action on the side." He walked out of the dressing room.

So that was it! What had Alby said the other night? "I've got a feeling it's gonna be big."

Unbelievable! What kind of fool does he take me for? All along it's been me doing the work, and him raking in the bucks. In the ring, it's been all me—not him. Me! And where's he at now?

Nowhere! He swung wildly at the air in front of him.

seventeen

With Tito the Titan down and one more to go before the Fence, Alby went over to the concession stand. He found a few takers. Most of the guys who'd bet earlier knew the Bear wasn't likely to lose. They were asking for outrageous bets. One man said, "I got a dime says your boy can't win in the first round again." Another said, "How does five dollars sound if you give me ten to one?" This was chump change, Alby thought. Nevertheless, he had to take just about every bet offered him to make any money now that he'd paid Ciro off. He thought, *I should've told Bare to take it easy on some of the other fighters to keep these guys guessing. Too late for that.* Plus, that would've given him away to Barry. *Maybe next time. Yeah, I like that—the next time.* He'd made a good chunk of cash today, so there'd have to be a next time.

Maybe he'd even set up similar events in the area too. He scanned the auditorium. Everybody here paid ten bucks at the door. There was money to be made with a crowd this size. It was worth thinking about.

But right then, with no one wanting to put real money on anybody going up against Barry, Alby had to raise the stakes. Give them something to nibble on, then they'd be hooked. "I'll take your ten; I'll take your five; who else wants some of this action?" They mumbled together. One guy said, "Even money—two bucks your guy won't knock out the other." Alby took it.

When it was time for this next match, the next to last, Alby met up with Barry and said, "Go for a quick kayo on this one, why don't you?"

"What for?"

"You've had a long day." His lip was quivering. He drank some water and wiped his mouth to cover it up. "Or maybe like a challenge for you. Keep you on your toes."

"Sure. I'll see what I can do, *manager*."

Alby's ears perked up—Barry, sarcastic? He made *manager* sound like something nasty. "Listen, Bare," he said. "I'm sorry. I didn't mean to put any pressure on you. Take all three rounds if you want. It's just I'm thinking that maybe you want to have as much rest before the final match as you can get. But do it any which way you can."

"Will do, then. But we need to talk. After."

"Sure. What about?"

"You know what about. The payout! A hundred bucks, a

T-shirt, a trophy, and a couple of coupons for Peter Piper Pizza. How do those coupons break down sixty-forty?"

Before Alby could answer, the ref called, "Barry 'The Bear' and Lee 'The Bull' Black!" The crowd cheered.

Alby stood speechless. He'd been busted.

If Barry lost this fight, Alby would be out the fifty covering his latest bets. Which meant no money for Barry, period. He left the ring and found a seat.

How could he explain this one? "Hey, Bare, my friend, my pal. I didn't tell you about the ridiculous prizes because . . . because why? I knew you'd win and I'd be laying bets on you all day long and we'd make out like bandits that way?" Or, if he wanted to be really honest, he could say, "Bare, my friend, my pal, there's one of you born every second."

No—he was the sucker. How much more stupid could he have been!

Alby had messed up royally this time. No smooth talking was going to get him out of this one. And maybe he shouldn't be looking for an easy out this time around. This was his best friend, and he had taken horrible advantage of him. With all Barry's hard work, Alby had practically nothing to show for it.

What a loser!

Who wasn't a loser was Barry. Good as Lee "The Bull" Black was, he looked sluggish and tired after two rounds. The third was more of the same: Barry's right hooks smacked hard against the Bull's side. The Bull grimaced and his hands kept dropping to his waist. That was when Barry caught him with a straight left to his nose. The Bull went down on a knee. Everybody was on their feet cheering the Bear on. The Bull was up after the count of five and waved Barry on.

He's got the heart of a fighter, Barry thought. They met in the middle of the ring, and the Bull threw a huge left upper-cut that missed. Barry had been waiting for this moment and he lost no time. He flicked two jabs right on the button, causing blood to gush from the Bull's nose, then he let go of a solid hook to the liver. The Bull collapsed where he was. The bell sounded and the fight was over. The Bull was able to push himself off the mat, and made his way to his corner. Barry went over to the Bull and said, "You're solid, man. Best all day long."

Alby stayed sitting. Through the schmucks in front of him, he saw Barry shaking the Bull's hand and scanning the crowd, looking for him, most likely. He sank down in the chair.

He slid out of his seat. Hunched over, he made his way to the concession stand to collect. *Good*, he thought, *I'm building up my pot again. It isn't much yet, but it will be. And Barry's jaw will drop when he sees it. He'll eat his words.*

Already the others were asking what odds he'd lay on the Fence match. They were willing to take almost anything he offered, but they were talking big money: bets starting out at a hundred bucks and up. What did they know that he didn't? Last second, he decided to play it conservative: even money, his man to win, nothing fancy. As quickly as he'd said so, he'd bet all the money he had.

If Barry won in the Fence, that would mean around four hundred and fifty. That could be enough, but Alby knew Barry had it in him to come out ahead, even against a pro. *I mean, what kind of pro would fight in this sort of event?* There was so much more cash to be made, so he jumped neck-deep into it, taking more bets than he knew he could cover.

Barry just had to win.

To be safe, Alby went into the dressing room. He tied the heavy curtain back to free up the pushbar on the exit. He checked: unlocked.

If Barry lost, Alby would have to run. Fast.

eighteen

In the dressing room, Barry's heart raced when he peered through the curtain and saw three men carrying a few rolls of chain-link fencing toward the ring. Even though the main event was called Fence o' Fighting, he'd thought it was a gimmick to get people to come out. He hadn't thought there'd be a real fence.

Something else Alby didn't tell me about.

The men unrolled their bundles of chain link and screwed them into the corner posts. When the eight-foot fence was up, the crowd went crazy screaming and cheering. From the sound of it, no one had left. The fight would be like any other today, straight-up boxing, but they didn't care. The fence was something different. An added element of danger. They were up on their feet.

The ref came into the locker room and explained to Barry, "The only ones allowed inside the cage are the two fighters and me, and between rounds, trainers can reach in to drop a stool, a bucket, and anything else the fighters need. Got it?"

Barry nodded.

Moments later, he stepped through an opening in the fence to find Mike "The Maniac" McDougal across from him in the ring.

Mike? But it was his show. Fair or unfair? Didn't matter now. *I've gotten this far on my own,* Barry boasted to himself. *I've got what it takes to finish it.* He shook out his arms, starting at the shoulders. That was why Mike had been in the dressing room carrying a gym bag. Now he stood waiting in shining gold fight trunks, shoes, head guard, and gloves.

Alby's mouth fell open. Mike! Standing there, staring Barry down, a slight smile on his face. And just about the meanest look Alby had ever seen. Meaner than Ciro. Meaner than the men he'd been betting against today. "Listen, Bare," Alby said through the fence, "this ain't right. The guy's not fought once today."

"So?"

"So this might not be worth it! What if you get hurt?"

Now it matters to you? "You saying he's better than me? What kind of manager are you?"

Whoa! Barry was steaming. Alby shook his head. "It's just—"

Barry got in Alby's face. "Just what?"

Alby's lips were trembling. "Nothing, Bare. I know you can handle him, so if you want to go through with it, let's do it."

"Let us do it? You mean me. Let me do it. Why don't you go take care of your business?"

Barry turned away. He was on his own in the ring. Had to rely on his skills, his own power. *Sixty-forty? Should be more like ninety-ten, and I'm being generous.* In the ring, he had no need for friends. Not friends like Alby, anyway.

Out of their corners, Mike and Barry danced around, measuring each other with jabs and feints; the crowd booed and hissed and screamed for a real fight. Barry's focus was off, way off. If all he was getting was a measly hundred, a shirt, and a couple of slices of pizza, why'd he been fighting all day long? Why'd Alby let him?

And so Mike caught Barry with a good hard right hook to the temple. The crowd cheered, up on its feet.

Alby winced at the solid hit. He slinked away from the ring and found a seat. He mapped out a path to the locker room and back door. He bit his fingernails. He'd taken over five hundred bucks' worth of bets beyond what he could cover on this fight alone.

For Barry, it took one shocking instant to feel his knees buckle, and then the brightest star he'd ever seen imploded in his brain. Blinding. He could taste the brightness too: iron mixed with mud. He must have closed his eyes, because it felt like he had to open them, and when he did, the split second before falling, he saw Pop in his face instead of Mike hopping from foot to foot, shadowboxing to keep warm, then charging at him with hard blows to ensure a knockout. It was Pop and him in the Galaxie, driving back from South Carolina: "You're okay, mi'jo. Shake it off. You're good."

"Pop," Barry said, shutting his eyes, trying to shake the webs loose. "Where are we?"

"Nearing the Georgia border."

"What . . . ?"

Then the bright star began to recede, disappearing into a pinpoint of dullness, and there was a throbbing in Barry's head, pounding on the back of his skull. It was the headrest. No, no, it was the mat. He heard the crowd cheering, Alby in the corner screaming, "Bare, Bare, are you okay?" Barry heard fear in Alby's voice, getting louder. He kept his eyes closed because what if he opened them and Pop was gone?

He'd seen Pop with his hands on the steering wheel, and heard Pop so clearly. If he scrunched up his eyes tight enough to see stars, he could still make out Pop's face, his knuckles, just barely hear his voice, the hum of the engine, and he wanted to stay in that place as long as possible. Forever. He wanted to ask Pop, "What should I do?" But way off in the distance, he heard the ref counting, the crowd yelling. Still, he kept his eyes shut tight.

Barry hadn't realized he missed Pop this much. He felt tears well up and begin to squeeze through his eyelids, then stream down the sides of his face. The tears trickled into his ears, and that felt funny. Like when he was a kid and Pop and him were shooting water guns at each other outside. Pop caught Barry from behind and said, "Now I've got you, mi'jo." He wrapped his arms around Barry and laughed, then he squeezed the trigger, shooting water straight into Barry's ear. After, Barry had to tilt his head to the side to make the water come out.

The memory was so vivid Barry didn't want to tilt his head to push out the tears. If he let go of them, he was afraid he would forget that time.

But what would Pop have said? "Get it together, mi'jo! Open your eyes, push yourself off the mat, do what you have to do where you're at. And remember, winning isn't winning if you're heart's in the wrong place." Then Pop's voice and face were gone.

Barry heard the ref: ". . . five . . ."

Alby screamed, "Get up, Barry. Get up!"

". . . six . . ."

Barry turned over onto his side, got up on an elbow. The tears streamed out of his ears.

"That's the way!" Alby yelled. "Up, up!"

The crowd was screaming.

"That's the way," Alby shouted.

". . . seven . . ."

Barry got up to one knee, then pushed himself off the canvas using his gloved fists. Up on his feet, just about.

". . . eight . . ."

Finally Barry opened his eyes. Standing in front of him, the ref said, "Show me the leather."

"What?"

"Your gloves, boy. Show them to me." The old man wiped dirt from the gloves onto his stomach. "You okay, young fella?"

Over the man's shoulder, the crowd was up on its feet, everyone cheering. For or against him, it didn't seem to matter. He couldn't tell anyway.

"I said, are you good to fight some more?" said the ref.

"Yeah, yeah, I am." Barry looked at Alby, grabbing hold of the corner post with one arm, his other hand gripping the fence. Alby was frantic with worry. *For me? Or for himself?* Right now that didn't matter. Barry was up, and Mike was bouncing from one shoe to the other, a sheen of sweat covering his chest, glaring.

"Let's fight, then, boys," the ref said from the center of the ring, slapping his hands together.

Mike came out of his corner in a flash, gloves up, head leaning forward slightly.

Out in the middle now, Barry put up his own gloves and blocked a couple of hard knocks from Mike with his forearms, then used them to push Mike off him. Both were huffing, snorting.

This was the longest minute of Barry's life.

Mike wanted to end it right here, right now. He charged in, looking for the clear shot. He jabbed, jabbed, stepped left, and again, to the face, to the face, and stepped right.

Before Mike changed his rhythm, Barry did some quick measuring. Between Mike's second jab and step right, he let go a left hook with a hint of an uppercut that caught Mike on the jawbone.

Mike hadn't seen it coming. His head snapped left and up, his eyes closed. Then his knees folded inward. He shook them straight and shook the cobwebs out of his head and smiled grimly; he was okay.

But Barry knew otherwise. His glove had come flush with Mike's head, he'd heard the snap of the neck, seen Mike's eyeballs go white. Then his eyes had rolled back down from somewhere high up in his head. He hadn't been able to focus, even when he was smiling. Pretending he was good to go, no problem.

The bell rang to end the round, and Barry went back to his corner. Alby was quiet and passed Barry a bottle of water through the opening. Barry sipped a tiny bit to keep his throat just wet enough, then spit the rest into the bucket Alby held out for him. He was breathing hard.

Alby passed him a towel, and he wiped his face, then draped it around his shoulders. Alby took ice wrapped in a hand towel and pushed it down on the back of Barry's neck. "We okay, Bare?"

Barry glared at him over his shoulder. "You tell me, Alby. Are we okay? Will Momma be okay? Or is she going to have to worry instead of taking that break you've been pushing for?"

What could Alby say? If Barry lost now, he'd be in for a ton of cash with a lot of guys who looked tougher than Ciro and his boys. Men who'd want their cash now, or they'd take him out to the dark alley and beat the life out of him. "Listen," he finally said, "if you think you can't go on—or if you don't want to because . . . It's your call. I'm with you."

Barry said, "Pretty slick, Alby. You almost had me going there."

"But . . . ," said Alby. He took back the ice pack, the water bottle, the bucket, and Barry stood. Alby took the stool.

The bell rang. Alby waited. What would Barry do? He breathed out heavy when Barry unwrapped the towel from around his shoulders.

"Let's get this over with. Later we can talk."

Alby held his hand out for the towel, but Barry threw it on the canvas.

Then he was back in the center of the ring, face to face with Mike the Maniac, who still seemed groggy. He was smiling a lot and jiggled his head back and forth, danced too much on the tips of his toes. Like a guy hurt but saying he wasn't.

Barry faked a right uppercut by cocking back his arm, his glove rubbing his own ribs, and he saw Mike flinch and back away. Then Barry shoved his left glove right at Mike's nose, which began to swell.

The Maniac smiled bigger and danced more wildly, all the while waving an open glove at the crowd and at Barry. He pounded on his heaving chest, then rubbed his nose with the back of his glove.

Mike shot tiny, fast jabs at the air in front of Barry's face, always pulling his fists back quickly to cover up, so Barry went for his chest and gut. Pop had told him to do this to get it done right: "Knock the wind out of him, again and again. One jab to the chest, then to the liver. Do it over and over, and the fight's done." Pop snapped his fingers. "It'll take some doing because there's no flash in this technique. A real fighter's got to have lots of patience. A crowd'll try to push a fighter into another kind of fight. Not too many folks in the audience like watching real boxing. They want the showboats; they want the windmill, roundhouse punchers. Wild, wild. Some fighters fall for that trap. They want to go for the knockout blow right out of the corner to please the crowd. A good fighter waits. Jabs hard at the sternum, then smack-dab at your guy's side, up at the chest again, to his liver. *Poom, poom, poom, bam.* It's a win every time."

That was how Barry handled Mike the rest of the second round.

At the bell beginning the final round, Mike stood in his corner, tried to raise his gloves to his chest, took a breath, and asked his corner man for something. The ref held Barry to his corner with a finger, then waved his arms in the air and went over to Mike, who'd sat back down on his stool. He sat gulping down water, taking deep, deep breaths.

Mike's gloves came off.

After a few long moments, the ref motioned for both fighters to meet him at the center of the ring. Mike was swaying left and right, shaking his legs loose. He looked up at Barry and then he stood stock-still, dropping his arms to his sides. He wouldn't look up at the crowd. Maybe it was because they were all shouting, "Bear, Bear, Bear!"

Barry tried hard to shut them out. It just didn't sound the same as before. Alby had messed up what should've been a good time.

"Settle down, now," the ref shouted, then raised his arms to quiet the audience.

"And the winner by technical knockout, the Rio Grande Valley's own Barry 'The Bear' Esquivel," he yelled, mispronouncing the last name, *Eskweevale*.

No matter. The day was finally over, and Barry'd won it all. Mike's corner man came into the ring carrying a gold trophy, a boxer holding up his arms in victory. He held it up and yelled, "And for winning not just every one of his own matches of the Man o' Might, but for also winning in the Fence o' Fighting bout, Barry the Bear gets this trophy. . . ." He handed it to Barry as folks began to file out the front.

The metal plate at the base read "Winner of the 2007 Man o' Might competition." The *2007* was in a different type than the rest of the text.

Then the announcer unfurled a T-shirt. It read, "I got all the way through the Fence o' Fighting match and all I got was this CRUMBY shirt." He held up Barry's left arm in victory.

The man pulled a crisp hundred-dollar bill from his shirt pocket, displayed it over his head, then handed it to Barry. "There you go, friend. And good doing today."

"So that's it?"

"Well," the guy whispered, "you get these coupons too. And the pride of knowing you beat Mike 'The Maniac' McDougal, a former pro fighter, at one time ranked number twelve in the world. That's something you can brag about to your grandkids. Otherwise, this is it." Then he shouted into the crowd, "Now, let's make some real noise for our champ. Put your hands together."

Those few left tried to be loud, but even they were turning to go. The boxing extravaganza was over. They'd head home and look forward to the next time. Maybe a few of them would try their hand at it to say they'd done it.

Barry stared at the bill. *All that work, and this is it. Wow.*

He gave the stragglers a quick wave. Alby was nowhere to be seen. So Barry stepped down from the ring, walked back to the dressing room, and sat down heavy. He dropped his winnings onto his bag. Ciro poked his head through the curtain. "My man, Bear," he said, flashing a wad of cash.

nineteen

By the time his buddy showed up, Barry was dressed. "So this is it?" He shoved the trophy at a smiling Alby. "I thought you said there was going to be big money involved? That we'd split the prize sixty-forty? I'd hand Momma some real cash?"

Alby bent and picked up the trophy.

"I'm sorry, Bare. I meant to tell you earlier about that, but . . ."

"Sure, yeah. Always there's a *but* with you. Always some excuse. So what now? I go home with that stupid trophy and this rag?" He flung the T-shirt at Alby, who let it drop to the floor. "You'll get your forty bucks tomorrow."

Alby cradled the trophy, looking at the shirt on the floor. "No. Keep it. You got this all wrong, Barry."

"Oh, yeah? Well, why don't you explain it to me so I'm clear, then."

"Listen, sure." Now he returned Barry's look. "I could've told you right off the bat about there not being any huge payout. What then? You probably wouldn't have fought. If you hadn't fought, you wouldn't have won like you did. And we would've lost the opportunity of a lifetime. You see . . ." He tried smiling.

"Opportunity of a lifetime?" Barry broke in. "Was that what this was to you? Is that what *I* am to you? The break you needed?"

"No, you just don't know. I had—"

"You don't have to tell me. After the fight, Ciro found me and told me everything. Bragging he'd won big off me today, and that you won enough from me in the first few fights to pay off what you owed him for losing at cards. Tell me, Alby, how much was it you won off me?"

"It doesn't matter, Barry. What does matter is I'm sorry. I should've told you, yeah, but who was thinking straight?"

"It doesn't matter the state of your mind, you should've come clean. But you didn't. Instead, you used me. I've always bent over backwards for you. What have you ever done for me? I can't remember a time. But you know what? You're right. It doesn't matter. What matters is that you used me. Worse, you abused our friendship."

Alby held the trophy back out to Barry, but Barry didn't take it. Alby looked him straight in the eye. "Maybe this'll help smooth things out." He pulled out a wad of bills from his pocket and unfolded it. "Look at it, Barry."

Barry didn't. He glared, so Alby shoved the clump of cash at Barry's chest. "Take it, man. Look, if it'll make it easier for you to forgive your old pal Alby, you take it all. It's over a thousand there. Won it all on the final match. It's all yours. Don't worry about our agreement. The whole chunk is yours. Give that to your momma and see how her face lights up." He smiled weakly. His hand was still out-stretched. How could Barry just pass up this much cash?

Yeah, Barry thought, *it would be great to get home, wrap up that wad in fancy paper, put a big purple bow on it, and hand it over to Momma.* But that hadn't been the deal between them. A hundred—that was the cash he'd fought for. This other thing had been Alby's deal. *He bet on* me. *He used* me. People would say he was nuts, but he wasn't touching it. Pop wouldn't have.

Barry would call Coach Pelfrey about the Galaxie to-morrow. It'd be Sunday. Coach could come over after church, and they'd talk numbers. Barry would take whatever Coach offered. He didn't need Alby's money.

Right now, he felt like shoving his fist in Alby's face. "Keep it. It's ill got. That's what *you* worked for. Not me. Here's a tip if you want to keep on gambling: don't bet on us staying friends."

"But, Barry, I did this for you, for your momma."

Barry got in Alby's face. He balled up his fists. "No,

Alby. You did this to get yourself out of the worst jam of your life. And that you did. You might have won a lot of money, but you've lost our friendship. I hope it was worth it." He turned to walk away, then looked over his shoulder: "That better be the last time you talk about Momma."

"Barry. Hey, Barry, don't. Let's talk some more."

Barry kept walking.

Alby said, "At least let me give you a ride back."

"I'm good on my own two feet."

❋

As Barry walked home, he wondered if he'd just made his stupidest move ever. A thousand dollars would've gone a long way in his house. Like Alby said earlier in the week: isn't it more wrong not to help your momma when you can?

What did Alby know?

Every time Barry started to feel good about his decision, a picture of Momma popped into his head. *What did I just do?* Technically, he had worked for that money.

He rubbed at the slight pain in his cheekbone. He knew it would hurt more tomorrow morning. His legs were weak; the bag felt like a load of cinder blocks hanging off his shoulder. He was tired and hungry. He wanted to be home already.

When he got in, Momma was at work, so he showered, ate, and went to bed still doubting himself.

twenty

Sunday morning, a little swollen in the face, his knuckles bruised and tender, his arms and legs rubbery, his ribs sore, Barry sat down to breakfast with Momma. They ate quietly across from each other.

"Are you okay?" she asked, peering at the redness on his cheekbones and cut on the upper lip.

"Nothing to worry about, Momma. Nothing an ice pack won't cure." He could tell by the way she wasn't looking at him, just eating, that she wanted to know how much he'd won but didn't want to seem ungrateful, or money-grubbing. "I won, Momma."

She smiled slightly, still not looking up.

"I beat every man they put in front of me, and not one hurt me, not really." He wouldn't say a word about him and

Pop in the Galaxie that brief moment when the Maniac cleaned his clock. But the punch hadn't hurt, so he wasn't lying. He'd just shaken it off. "I even won the main event against their ringer. The Battle in the Fence o' Fighting, they called it." He laughed.

Momma's smile widened. "I knew all along you would. Even so, I was so worried the whole day, mi'jo. Alby called in the morning and again in the late afternoon before I went to work to let me know that you were okay, and winning."

That was nice, calling. Sometimes that boy surprises me, he thought. *But no matter.* Alby'd still made a sucker of him. Was that what had been bothering him all along? That he wasn't the man he thought he needed to be, that he could be taken advantage of so easily? When he should've known better? And he was supposed to be the man of the house?

Momma looked up, and he saw the question in her eyes. How could he tell her he'd won every match but gotten almost nothing? And what would she think of him not taking the thousand?

"Well, I'm happy to see you're okay. You need anything? Some aspirin? That ice pack?"

"No thanks. All in a day's work."

"What's the matter, then? For having won, you seem awfully glum."

"I'm sorry, Momma."

"What for? Your pop would've been beaming proud of you, you know that?"

"You think so?"

"I do. Sure, it wasn't the Olympic trials or the Golden Gloves, but he would've been jumping for joy, carrying you on his shoulders—his Barry, the champ."

"Maybe, but he would've still been all down in the mouth and saying to me, 'I told you so, mi'jo.'"

"Told you what?"

"What I'm really and truly sorry about, Momma. I raised your hopes; my own, too. Alby threw some pretty words at me, and I fell for them, again. He made a chump of me, Momma."

"What do you mean?" When he didn't answer, she took her plate to the sink. "You want seconds, baby?"

"No thanks. I'm good." He patted his stomach. He wiped his plate clean with the last piece of tortilla. Her back was to him. He could see her shoulders rising and falling. "I'm sorry, Momma. But I fought for nothing. Well, not for nothing. I did get sixty dollars, and *that*," he said, and pointed at the prizes next to the trash can.

She picked up the trophy. "Wow!" she said, trying to sound excited. "This is great, Barry. Maybe we can take it to that place at the mall and have your name engraved on it. What do you say?" She faced him. "Wait. What was it doing by the trash can?"

"Toss it, Momma. It's plastic. It's one of maybe hundreds these guys pass out in any town they go to. It's not a week or two of time off with no worries for you like I hoped. It's just plastic. It's stupid."

She picked up the shirt, too, unfurling it, and giggled when she read it. "Mi'jo, this is a trophy; it's something," she said, holding the figurine up. "The shirt, on the other hand, is ridiculous. But I like it. Can I keep it?"

Barry laughed and so did she. "It's yours if you're so stuck on it."

"I am," she answered, and left the kitchen. He knew she was clearing a space for the trophy on the mantel next to Pop's photos of Fabian. She'd make certain that anybody who dropped in took notice. She'd say, "My Barry won it for being the champ. He won every fight that day. The real deal of a champ."

She came back in wearing the T-shirt, and he laughed.

"What do you think?" She twirled around. "I like it for around the house."

"Sure, Momma, as a dustrag—but it's yours. It's the least I can give you."

She smiled.

"Momma."

"Yes?"

"I think I did something bad, though."

"What? Are you sure you're okay?"

"Sure, Momma. Well, I don't know. It's that Alby won all kinds of money betting on the fights. I didn't know he was doing it. Didn't find out till way at the end. After the fights, he told me I could have it all, if I wanted. I told him no. I turned down a thousand dollars, Momma."

She looked startled. Then she reached for his hand.

"That's a lot, but you did the right thing. Pop hated gambling. We're not broke yet."

"Are you sure? Are we going to be okay?"

"Sure we are. We'll have a garage sale. Sell anything we don't need or that's not nailed down. Except for this T-shirt! And the grocery store's looking for some part-timers. First chance I get tomorrow, I'll go out there and—"

He cut her short. "No, Momma, you won't. Coach Pelfrey's coming over later to see about the Galaxie, if that's okay by you."

"But, mi'jo?"

"I think it's time for us to move on. Selling the car's the first step forward. You know, Pop would want it that way."

"But—"

"We need to go to church now. You're not going to wear that, are you?" They both smiled.

She had tears in her eyes, so Barry hugged her and whispered, "Everything's going to work out. I know it. This time no one's making a fool of me. My word is my honor."

Later, after talking with Coach, Barry would go deliver Alby's share of the prize money and be done with it.

✳

About the time the Esquivels were leaving for church, Alby was getting downstairs for breakfast. Dad was into his second cup of coffee, reading the paper.

Alby sat and reached for the milk and cereal. He hadn't

slept much. Last night, he'd hidden the money in a box and slipped it under his bed. Then he lay down and cried, actually shed tears, because he'd been about the stupidest person in the world. He'd lost his best and only true friend, and now there was no talking smooth enough to find a way out of this mess.

Dad folded over the paper. "You okay, son? You look dead tired. What's on your mind?"

"Nothing much," he said, hoping that would be enough to get Dad back to reading. But Dad kept staring at him. Alby shoved a spoonful of cereal into his mouth. "What?"

"Here's something interesting," Dad said. He pushed the sports page over. "Look."

Alby glanced at the paper. It was a photo of him and Barry after the Fence match. Barry was being handed the trophy. Alby was standing off to the side, frowning. It must have been taken right before he went to collect. He hadn't even realized the paper was covering the event, much less taking pictures. Alby nodded halfheartedly.

"I almost skipped over it. Except one thing caught my attention. How sad one of the boys looked. And it was you! I wanted to know what in the world you two were doing at this sort of event. More than that, I wanted to know why Barry was in the ring. Did Mrs. Esquivel know about it? And what did Barry get you into?"

"It's nothing, Dad. We were just messing around."

"Messing around? The paper says Barry was in some five fights plus the main event. That doesn't sound like just messing around to me. So talk to me, Alby. If nothing else, tell me this—if Barry won it all, why do you look so miserable now and in the picture?"

Had he heard right? *Me talk to him? Not the other way around?* He didn't think he knew how. But this thing with Barry . . . "Like I said," Alby started, then he broke down crying for no reason. He just couldn't control himself. He was hysterical, going on about how he'd done about the dumbest thing in the world he could do, taken advantage of his best friend to pay Ciro back for poker, and the rest of it. "Why wouldn't he take the money, Dad? He earned it. And worse, I don't have him for a best friend anymore. All because I couldn't see another way out but to gamble more and more."

Dad seemed confused by everything Alby had just blubbered. He got up and stood behind Alby, hands on his shoulders. "It's all okay, son," he kept whispering. "Calm down. Tell me again, slowly. We'll try to work it all out. We'll draw up a plan of action. What we can't fix quick, well, we'll work hard to get right. You've got to keep a stiff upper lip. We're winners in this family, not quitters. So let's act like it."

But, man, Alby didn't feel like a winner. He couldn't see a way out of this mess. Though it did feel good to be held this way. Why hadn't they been like this before? Would they keep it up?

Alby cried because all these years he'd thought Mom and Dad couldn't care less about him. But here Dad was gripping him, his voice cracking even, like he was also crying. This was one of those times that Alby had always seen between Barry and his pop, and every time, deep down in his heart, he wished the same thing would happen for him and Dad.

So he cried some more, because everything would be all right. Dad had said so. He knew it as certain as Dad was standing behind him, holding him. This moment should stretch on forever. Like when Alby was a kid and he'd ask, "How much do you love me?"

"As far as I can stretch my arms," Dad would say, "and then just beyond my fingertips. Far, far, and forever."

epilogue
. . . closer than a brother

Two months after the fights, Barry held true to his word. First, after he sold the Galaxie to Coach, he made sure Momma took a week off from her day job. But it wasn't all fun and games. She cleaned the house spotless, rearranged the living room furniture, and went looking for work every day, before going to her night job.

Barry tried to get her to slow down. "Momma, we're going to be all right. We've got enough money now." She shook her head and said, "Save it." He put the money into a savings account. Eventually Momma found a job that replaced the other two. She was the secretary to the boss at the tennis shoe factory. Full-time, health insurance and other benefits. And she got some overtime. Barry convinced her to let him work the summer full-time at the Dairy Queen, then go to part-time in the fall, when he'd enroll at the community college. He'd study auto mechanics, following in Pop's footsteps. At the same time, he'd take his basic courses and later transfer to the university.

The second way he kept his word was to stay clear of Alby. Maybe one day he'd see past how disappointed he was in his old friend. But to be used like that, to be made a fool of . . . Barry just didn't know. He hung out with the kids at the DQ. He even asked one of the girls, Emma, on a date. They went to a movie, then to a park, where he pushed her on a swing. They were still going out. So it wasn't a bad summer, but Barry was still upset. Lately he'd started to blame himself more for his own foolishness. Alby was Alby, and he couldn't be anyone else. But Barry was supposed to be smarter about these things. At least, he hoped he was, and not the idiot he felt like now.

Maybe someday Barry would tell Alby how he was at fault too, so could they still be friends. Say he was sorry for overreacting. But had he, really? Or was he just making excuses because he missed his buddy? What was it the counselors at school called someone who no matter the circumstances helped a friend to keep doing bad stuff, like drugs or drinking, or in this case, gambling? An enabler.

He'd behaved badly too. He'd been full of pride, thinking he was some kind of hot-shot boxer because he went 6–0. What had he thought back then? *It's me in the ring. Nobody else. ME!* How egomaniacal was that? That kind of thinking was as bad as gambling. He'd have to apologize to Alby for that too.

He couldn't figure it all out. One thing he did know, he missed Alby something fierce. His constant jabbering about everything and nothing. That goofy way he had of punching the bag in the garage.

Every day, Barry would pull out the silver pen, look at the inscription, and think, *Champ? More like chump.*

A week or two into summer vacation, he heard Alby was mowing lawns in the neighborhood. At first, Barry thought this was another way Alby was making fun of him, cutting into his own work. Then Momma told him, "Oddest thing, mi'jo. I heard Alby's mowing several of the old folks' yards in the neighborhood for free."

What Momma didn't know was that Alby and his dad had done some serious figuring about how he could try to make things right. Alby had made a total of twelve hundred and fifty dollars on the fights, give or take. That meant if he mowed six lawns a week over the two and a half months of the summer at the going rate of twenty dollars per yard, he'd work enough to have really earned his winnings. He approached six of the neighborhood's older people and offered to work for free. They all wanted to know the strings attached; they suspected something because wasn't he the same Alby Alonzo from a couple of streets down who— "Well, you know," they all said.

He told them, "I know I've done some stupid stuff over the years to get you to think that of me. But you have to trust me; I'm on the up-and-up. Just give me a chance to prove myself." When they did, he worked hard and without complaining.

At summer's end, Barry heard a knock on the door.

Alby looked through the screen. "Listen, I understand if you want to tell me to take a hike, but before you do, I need to tell you something."

Barry remained quiet just inside the door. Alby looked softer through the mesh.

"Barry, I'm sorry. You'll never know how bad I feel for doing what I did to you. I took advantage of our friendship. I don't really deserve it, but I'm asking for your forgiveness."

Barry hoped Alby couldn't tell that tears were forming in his eyes. Alby's voice made him feel like the wind had been knocked out of him. They hadn't talked in such a long time. And this was an altogether different Alby. What he said seemed to come from deep inside.

"Now understand," Alby said, and pulled an envelope from his pocket, "this is not to be taken as a means to buy my way out of anything, or a bribe. But you need to know, I'm a changed person; I'm trying to do my best to be a man of my word. This is seven hundred fifty dollars. Your sixty percent from the fights. I earned it this time." He was silent. "Besides this, I've got nothing—my sincerest apology and my word is all."

Barry pushed open the door and draped his heavy arms around Alby's neck. He was crying. "No, no. I'm the sorry one. We're supposed to be best friends. I shouldn't have shut you out like I did. We could've talked."

Alby was crying too. "You can't know," he said, "what a load off this is."

But Barry did know. With true friendship, when it got hard, a guy worked to get it right. Alby had done his part in coming over today. Barry hugged him hard and said, "It's all good, Alby. It's all so good now."

He scrunched up his eyes, and that same weight lifting off Alby's shoulders was lifting off his, too, and it felt like the entire heavens full of stars was shooting across the sky. Across the sky streaks of never-ending light. He kept his eyes closed for a few more seconds. He didn't ever want to forget this moment.

about the author

René Saldaña, Jr., teaches in the College of Education at Texas Tech University in Lubbock, where he lives with his wife, Tina; their sons, Lukas and Mikah; and their cat, ISBN. He is the author of *The Jumping Tree* and *Finding Our Way: Stories*. His work has also appeared in *Face Relations: 11 Stories About Seeing Beyond Color, Guys Write for GUYS READ, Every Man for Himself: Ten Stories About Being a Guy, Make Me Over: 11 Original Stories About Transforming Ourselves, Boys' Life,* and *READ,* among other publications. He's a big fan of boxing but hates gambling.